Lock Down Publications and Ca$h
Presents

I0658212

PROBLEM SOLVED 2

Die, B*tch, Die

Written By
Christopher "Diesel" Hornezes

CHRISTOPHER "DIESEL" HORNEZES

First Edition 2025

Printed in the United States of America

This is a work of fiction. Names, characters, places, and incidents either are products of the author's imagination or are used fictitiously. Any similarity to actual events or locales or persons, living or dead, is entirely coincidental.

Lock Down Publications
P.O. Box 944
Stockbridge, GA 30281
www.lockdownpublications.com

Like our page on Facebook: Lock Down Publications
www.facebook.com/lockdownpublications.ldp

By: Christopher A. Hornezes #704976
Racine Correctional Institution
P.O. Box 189
Phoenix, MD 21131

Stay Connected with Us!

Text **LOCKDOWN** to 22828 to stay up-to-date with new releases, sneak peaks, contests and more…

Like our page on Facebook:
Lock Down Publications

Join Lock Down Publications/The New Era Reading Group

Visit our website:
www.lockdownpublications.com

Follow us on Instagram:
Lock Down Publications

Email Us: We want to hear from you!

Chapter 1

9 Days Later
SMACK!

"Bitch, where the fuck are my diamonds?" Paula screamed, furious that she couldn't make a pregnant woman break. *"Where the fuck is my shit? I want my diamonds!"*

Bunz *refused* to show the Italian bitch any weakness, despite how much the sting of her hand smacking her in her already beat-up face hurt.

SMACK!

Her head snapped to the side from the source but turned right back to Paula. Looking into her eyes Bunz laughed, showcasing a mouth full of bloody teeth. She spit a wad of saliva mixed with blood at the other woman's Gianvito Rossi's but still didn't speak.

"You know what? I been playing with you for nine days, hopin' I wouldn't have to go this route, but you give me no choice. Now I'ma turn savage on you, stupid-ass cunt."

Paula went to the little table in the small concrete dungeon she had Bunz held prisoner in and grabbed a long razor-sharp knife. Bunz's heart dropped when what Paula grabbed.

"I hope you like fried baby, bitch, 'cause I'ma cut that bastard outta your belly, drop him in a pot of hot cookin' grease and I'ma *force* you to eat him like a fuckin' hamster eats her young!"Paula marched up to her and drew the blade

4

back, ready to slash open Bunz's exposed belly, when Bunz screamed in panic.

"Okay! Okay! I'll get your fucking diamonds! I'll get them just leave my fuckin' babies alone you evil bitch!"

"Babies?" Paula questioned, a sadistic grin growing on her face like a slick-ass bitch with a demented plan. "Hmmmm. More than one; no wonder why your belly is so big. I guess now, I have two ways to get what I want. Tell me where they are, bitch, or you're getting' a C-section without anesthesia!"

"In my condo! They're in my safe!" Bunz told her.

Paula went to the door and opened it. She called to her men that had been posted outside of the room. Bunz then saw three guys enter behind Paula.

"Untie this bitch; we're taking a trip to Chicago."

"I need to use the bathroom before we go," Bunz told her.

"You're beat. Hold it," Paula replied as Bunz was untied.

"Bitch! I'm fuckin' *pregnant*, and I have to take a shit! Do you really want me to shit on myself in yo' car? You know how bad pregnant doo-doo smells?"

Paula curled her lip up in disgust. "One of y'all take the bitch to the bathroom," she said, "and if she farts before she gets there, shoot her."

Standing up from the old steel chair she'd been tied to, barefoot wearing only a bra, and a pair of leggings, Bunz limped ahead when one of the taller guys in Paula's crew gestured her towards the doorway. She limped past him, clutching her big belly, casting a mean-mug at Paula on the way out.

***

"Don't take all fuckin' day," the guy told her, as he held the door open.

Bunz limped past him, stepping into the bathroom. She turned to him, catching his attention.

5

"Look, dude. That bitch is gon' kill me *and* my babies no matter what so why don't you do me a solid and let a bitch get one last nut off before I get put 6-feet deep," Bunz said to him.

The guy's eyebrows furrowed. "Come again?"

Bunz sucked her teeth, "Nigga, is you dumb? I *said*, I want you to fuck me before I die! Or are you a part of that *new-age* thing that's goin' on all over the world?"

"Hell naw I'm not gay! I love pussy!"

"Then step in and hit this pussy real quick. Everyone deserves to buss they last one before death comes for them."

He looked at her for a second, weighing his options. He, like most men, had fantasies about fucking thick Black women. Her exotic Asian-like face gave her such an exotic look. She had long dread locks that were gold like the sun. Standing 5'8, her rich caramel skin was deliciously flawless; she had succulent 36 DD cup breasts which looked even plumper due to her pregnancy. Her waist was naturally slim, and her hips were wide. Behind her was 48-inches of fat, round, juicy ass that bounced like it was filled with Jell-O when she walked. Her thick thighs and her toned running legs completed her. All her natural beauty was compliments of her mixed heritage of Jamaican, Puerto Rican, and Cambodian.

The 25-year-old was close to becoming a mother for the first time, but with the looks of things, Bunz knew that she had to do something… fast.

"Maaaan, what the fuck is you waitin' on?" Bunz snapped.

The man then pushed her all the way into the bathroom, closed the door, and locked it.

"You want some of this Italian sausage, bitch?" he asked her, unholstering his gun and setting it on the sink before undoing his pants. "Come on and put my cock in your mouth first, cunt!"

He dropped his pants and boxers to his ankles and pointed for her to take his hard 7-inches into her mouth. Bunz glanced at his gun. The sink wasn't too far away from her but, unfortunately, it was behind him.

"Come on, come on, come on! Let's go!"

In a matter of seconds, Bunz had an idea of how she could get up out of there, but it was unorthodox. She hardened herself up to do it. Her babies' lives depended on it. She went to the man and dropped down to her knees.

"Open up, whore," he demanded, holding his dick with one hand.

Bunz obeyed and opened her mouth wide for him. He stuffed his cock into her mouth, grabbed her head, and started fucking her face; groaning, cursing, grunting, eyes rolling to the back of his head.

"Oohhh *fuck*, yeah! Suck this dick, bitch," he told her, loving the bliss. "Your mouth feels so fucking good! I can't wait to stick my cock in your ass!"

Bunz gagged as his dick went down her throat repeatedly. Tears filled her eyes as she thought about Eric, lying face down on the ground, after Paula shot him. She didn't even care that her man had fucked the bitch. Bunz was sure that Paula had managed to seduce her fiancé, all a part of her plans to find her.

That was enough to make her start seeing red. On top of that this white man was face fucking her, on her knees, with two babies growing in her stomach and no regard for her life. That shit had her hot. Filled with a rage so intense that it burned like an out of control fire. That burn she felt was enough to give her the motivation she needed to handle her business.

The guard's eyes remained closed as he continued enjoying the feeling of her warm wet mouth. His bliss soon turned to discomfort, which turned into pain.

"Hey… hey, hey, hey! What are you… *Aaaagh owwwww!"* he screamed.

7

Infuriated and not giving a fuck, Bunz bit down on his dick as hard as she could. Her teeth sliced right through his flesh. He screamed in agony, his hands raised up, not knowing what the fuck to do.

"Stop, stop, stooop! Get off!" he begged as she chomped down harder.

Blood squirted all over her face as she ruptured him. In a last effort to completely immobilize the guy Bunz yanked her head hard to the left, then the right, then she yanked it back. She ripped his cock off, leaving a jagged tear at the base.

The guy fell backwards to the floor, screaming and crying, trying to hold his torn stump as blood spurted from the hole. He bled so much, so fast. Bunz hurried to get to her feet. She spit the severed dick out of her mouth and ran for the gun, grabbing it just in time to hear banging at the door.

***

"Go! Go! Get that bitch! Now!" Paula screamed when she and her men heard the blood-curdling screams come from the bathroom.

The six that were at her side ran off to go see what was going on. Paula grabbed her Ruger 5.7 out of her big Louis Vuitton handbag and followed with a full clip of armor-piercing rounds. Last in the line, she bent the corner then paused where she stood, looking up the hall. She saw one of the six men kick the bathroom door in.

BOCKA!

The man's head snapped back as a bullet slammed into his forehead. His brains flew out of the gaping hole in the back of his head, painting the wall behind him crimson. Paula gasped when she saw his body hit the floor, dead.

"Get her! What they fuck are you waiting for?" she screamed, clutching her pistol tightly in her hands.

Two others jumped into the path of the doorway and fired recklessly into the bathroom. They dumped ten shots each, then ceased fire. One stepped close to the doorway, to see if either of them had hit her. He took a step forward and, suddenly, was struck in the face with a bloody object. The other guy saw it was a severed dick and jumped back.

BOCKA! BOCKA! BOCKA! BOCKA! BOCKA! BOCKA! BOCKA!

Shots flew from the bathroom, taking them out while distracted by the bit-off cock. Both dropped to the floor, bleeding through all the holes in their chests. Finally, the last three attempted to run to the bathroom and just shoot until they got her. A hand gripping a pistol bent outwards around the doorway threshold and started firing. With no cover, the three remaining men were hit and dropped to the floor, dead.

Paula's heart pounded as she stood frozen in fear. She looked at her squad of so-called henchmen, stunned that six big, trained security guards had failed to take out a pregnant chick.

Who the fuck is this bitch? Paula wondered to herself.

A second later, she saw her, step out of the bathroom, with blood smeared around her mouth. Paula locked eyes with the girl, the one that had stolen hundreds of millions of dollars in rare and vintage diamonds and diamond jewelry from her father, then killed him *and* her mother. The chick looked demented, her long gold dreads all over the place, her mouth covered with crotch blood, and the fire in her eyes.

Paula shrieked when the girl raised her gun up and pointed it at her. She dropped the gun and took off running, terrified, like a woman that had a gigantic man on her ass trying to take what didn't belong to him.

***

Bunz pointed the gun and aimed at the back of Paula's head. She pulled the trigger.

CLICK CLICK CLICK CLICK CLICK
"Fuuuck!" she screamed, as Paula escaped sure death when her gun clicked empty. Bunz saw her bend the corner and disappear, her heels click-clacking the only thing she could hear as the petrified chick got further and further away. *"You're dead bitch! I will find you and when I do I swear to God I'm going to fucking kill you."*

Bunz heard one of the men choking. Quickly, she dropped the empty gun and grabbed another, cocking it. She saw which one of the men it was and pointed the pistol at him as he clung to life. Through glazed eyes, he glared up at her.

"G… G… Give up… it's… it's over," he managed to say to her.

Bunz curled her lip up in anger. She stared down into his eyes, stepping over to him, pointing the gun right at the center of his face.

"It ain't over 'til the bitch *dies*!" she declared then she put three in his face, shutting him the fuck up forever.

Bunz stared at the dead man for a minute. She then put one in the rest of their heads, making sure their eyes never opened again. She wiped the blood from around her mouth and limped off, clutching her belly.

"Hold on, babies. Mommy's getting us the hell out of here," she said to her unborn twins.

Minutes later, she found the exit and burst through it. When she stepped out, she discovered that she was in the woods somewhere.

Taking a deep breath, she got to walking, barefoot, with no intentions of stopping until she reached civilization. As she walked all she could thing about was that bitch Paula. Paula's face was forever burned into her mind and would be until she burned the bitch's face from it. She had taken the love of her life, the father to her twin son and daughter, her best friend. She had worked hard to prove to him that she wasn't some hood rat that came and went as she pleased and that she didn't put money over him. Tears rolled down her face as she limped into the thick brush.

I failed you, Eric, but I swear to God, I am going to get that bitch, and I am going to make her wish she was never born, Bunz thought to herself as she grew even angrier than she had when she bit the body guard's dick off.

It was on.

Chapter 2

5 Months Later

"Aye! What is this? You call that sauce? Huh? What the fuck makes you think that there's *anything* Italian about this? You're supposed to be making mushroom sauce! Not crap!" snapped Anthony, the owner of *Sapore d'Italia,* one of the most exclusive Italian eateries in downtown Chicago. *"Fix it or get the fuck out of my kitchen!"* he then screamed.

The hefty man, who was like an overweight version of Gordon Ramsey marched off, cursing in Italian, *so* very angry at the cooking skills of his newest chef. Andrea tried to keep from crying. She'd been yelled at nearly all 23 years she had been alive but it hurt bad when she was trying to do something legit with her life, rather than going back to her former life as a street walker.

The other chefs, produce preppers, and the dessert makers stayed working busily. Nobody wanted to piss the boss off. Nobody wanted to hear his mouth. Andrea wiped away the tears and dumped the sauce out to try again.

"Hey, 'Drea. Don't let that fat bastard get to you, girl."

Andrea turned to her left and saw the beautiful chef there at her side, giving her an encouraging smile. The woman was stunning. She had the milkiest white skin, with jet-black hair that was pulled up into a high ponytail on her head. Her face was that of an Asian's. She was taller than most females, standing about 5'8, even in the flats she had on her feet. The black chef pants she was wearing did nothing to hide to her thick thighs nor the big round fat juicy ass that had all the employees asking where she got that from. They all swore she *had* to have Black in her.

"He's just an asshole that probably doesn't get any pussy," the girl added, playfully nudging Andrea's side.

The young Italian couldn't help but to giggle at that. "Thanks, Geneva," Andrea replied. "He gets on my damn nerves. I'm just tryin' to be the best I can be."

"This ain't the Army, girl. Fuck him and his piss-poor attitude. Get cho' money and move on to the next day," Geneva replied. "Now we have a big event comin' up in about an hour. Let's get this shit together so we ain't gotta here his mouth no more tonight nor none of these *so-called* mobster people."

Finding that she loved how ghetto and hood that Geneva talked, Andrea nodded her head, then she walked off to get back to work. She dumped out the failure in the bowl she had gotten yelled at about, grabbed the ingredients to start over, and got to it.

***

An hour later, the kitchen smelled like one that was in Italy. The garlic from the buttery toasted bread slices filled the air, along with sauces, meats, and pastas. Everyone's mouths were watering at their creations.

Waiters and waitresses grabbed plates of perfectly proportioned meals and hurried them out to the guests, while others filled glasses and flutes with wines and champagnes. It was just after 9 'clock on a Friday night. The night was young. Plenty more hungry Italians were expected to show up.

"Andrea! Geneva! Raquel!"

The three ladies heard Anthony yell their names. They were standing outside of the kitchen, watching the guests dine on their exquisite cooking, when they saw their boss marching towards them. Andrea groaned, thinking he had yet another bone to pick with them.

"Hey! You three, come with me now! I've got a table that wants to meet you right now," Anthony told them, a smile growing on his face. "They love their food and they wanna meet the people who cooked it! Come on!"

The ladies followed him out onto the floor to where there was a big round table in the center of the restaurant. Andrea could tell that the people sitting there were very important, because Anthony never sat normal guests there.

There were eight people in total, two older women and two older men, with varying degrees of grey hair yet not a wrinkle in sight, and two young women and the same for young men who looked like they had never been told no a day in their lives.

Anthony gestured them to step up when they got to the table. He started introducing them to the people.

"Mr. Paulmatti, Mrs. Paulmatti," he said to the two that looked like they were as slick as snot and stuck up a horse's ass, "this is Chef Raquel, who has been my head chef for years; here we have my second-in-charge; Chef Geneva, and third, is my newest Chef Andrea." Anthony turned to the three as they all got head nods and smiles from the older folks, but eye rolls and smirks from the younger ones. "Ladies, please meet the Paulmatti family. There are in Chicago from California and chose my place to fill their stomachs with real Italian food. Thanks to you, they have been given the experience that they desired."

The chefs all nodded their heads and thanked the family for the compliments they all received when Anthony finished kissing ass. While the talkative man continued brown-nosing, Andrea peeped Geneva staring at one of the girls at the table. She looked at the chick herself.

She looked young, like she was in her early 20s; she had jet-black hair, milky white skin, and the face of a beautiful girl who thought nobody else could rival her glamor. She

14

was dressed in a black form-fitting one-shoulder dress that was covered in sequins. Her makeup made her look like a spoiled high-school brat, and her diamond jewelry did *not* look fake.

Andrea instantly developed a dislike for the chick that she was sure was stuck up. She leaned a little closer to Geneva and spoke so that only she could hear her.

"Do you know that girl?" she asked.

Geneva shook her head. "Nope," she said, but was still looking at the girl.

"Maybe you should stop staring at her, before we don't get our tip."

Geneva chuckled. "Thanks for the advice, 'Drea."

Suddenly, the sounds of a woman screaming caught everyone's attention. Andrea looked to her left at where the line of tables lining the interior walls of floor-to-ceiling windows were. A mob of men in masks and hoodies were pointing AK-47s at the restaurant.

People sitting at the tables all saw them and immediately tried to get up and run.

The men opened fire. Swarms of 7.62mm rounds exploded through the glass, shattering all of them and attacking the guests like frenzied Africanized killer bees. So many tried to get out of the lines of fire, but as the men advanced on the restaurant, the chance for escape dwindled.

Heads were steadily exploding. Body parts flew everywhere. Brains and bone fragments covered the floor. Blood splattered all over the walls.

Andrea screamed when bullets struck Anthony and Raquel. They were blown apart in mere seconds, reduced to a pile of bloody chunks of meet on the floor.

The members of the Paulmatti family all hopped up and drew pistols from their hand bags and waist lines. They started firing back at the mob.

Bullets flew in every direction. Andrea was so frozen in fear that she literally couldn't move. She was then hit hard from the side by someone and taken down to the floor. She looked up and discovered that it was Geneva on top of her.

"What the hell is going on?" she yelled over the deafening gun shots.

"My guess is the Paulmatti family has a target on their back and is about to die," Geneva yelled back.

The chaos continued. Andrea put her hands over her ears. It was so loud, like a war movie with movie-theatre quality sound, turned all the way up. Geneva looked up and saw that three of the shooters had focused on the girl she was staring at. Andrea swore that she could hear Geneva rooting for them, chanting, *Get her! Get that bitch!*

The four older folks caught hot ones to their chests and faces when they chose the wrong moment to hop up from where they had been ducked down for cover. The masked shooters blew them down with ease.

The two younger men jumped up firing at the shooters. It was completely useless as the bullets bounced off the armor and the Paulmatti boys were dropped by the flying bullets. More Paulmatti men tried firing but it was all useless. One person tried to run and was damn near cut in two as the bullets from the AK's ripped through his spine.

The three girls were ducked out of the way, gripping their semi-autos tightly, waiting for a chance to shoot and flee. The shooters began to advance on them, choppers pointed, eyes trained on where they knew the girls were hiding. One jumped up and tried to shoot.

BRRRRRRRRRRRRRRRRRR!

Down she went, with no upper body. The second held her hand up over the edge of the table and started firing. She caught one of the shooters in his leg, making him hit the floor, screaming in pain. Four of the other shooters opened fire at the table, sending enough bullets at it that the table split and she was annihilated.

They were just about to finish the job, when gun fire erupted from outside of the restaurant. They all turned towards the entrances they made and found themselves now the targets as an even bigger mob of armed Italians that had snuck up and started shooting AR-15s.

Not a single one of the masked goons had a chance to get out of the way. The Italians blew them all down like a professional bowler hitting a strike like it was easy. Andrea heard Geneva gasp while still held down on the floor by her. She herself was shocked at what she was seeing with her own eyes. Speechless, they both continued to watch as bullets flew and bodies dropped.

"Paula!"

Andrea saw a man hurry into the restaurant just then. She looked up and saw that he was not dressed like one of the other Italians. This man, olive complexioned, looked like a GQ magazine cover model. His thick black hair was slicked back, face clean-shaven. His suit looked custom-made, and he wore leather loafers on his feet. He gripped a Desert Eagle in his hand, with a frantic look on his face as he yelled again.

Just then, Andrea caught a glimpse of the young girl from the Paulmatti table hop up from where she had been hidden. She saw the guy and screamed his name.

"Rubio," Paula Paulmatti ran to the man and threw herself into his arms. He kissed her forehead as Paula begged, *"Get me out of here. Please take me home!"*

Without a word he nodded and gestured behind him. Two of his men ran over and guided her out of the restaurant. Rubio didn't follow, instead him and his remaining men went over to the bodies of the masked men. He crouched down and pulled one of the men's mask off. When he saw the shooter was Black, Rubio's lip curled up as if he was looking at someone's bowel movement in a McDonald's toilet.

"Pezzo di merda nero!," he spat, calling a piece of shit, then adding the N-word. racistly.

Andrea and Geneva heard him speak in Italian. Andrea knew exactly what he said and it made her so angry that she

17

nearly contemplated hopping up and rushing the guy to try and knock his jaw off.

Suddenly, he turned his head and looked directly at them. Andrea shrieked when he locked eyes with her. Geneva yanked on her and whispered through clenched teeth into her ear. "Don't show fear! *Ever*," she warned Andrea.

Rubio put a finger to his lips, looking at them and gave them a stern "*Shhhhh*," before he turned his head back to the shooter. Standing back upright, he cocked his pistol and pointed it directly at the goon's face.

BOC! BOC! BOC! BOC! BOC! BOC!

Andrea jumped from the sound of the close-range gunshots. She and Geneva saw the top of the goon's head blow off and his brains explode out of it onto the floor. Rubio then looked at them once more.

"*Shhhhhh*," he warned again then, with his crew following behind, he left out of the restaurant, disappearing from Andrea's and Geneva's line of sight.

Chapter 3

An hour after the Chicago police and detectives came and did a thorough investigation on the few people that were still alive, Andrea was still shaking with fear. Coming so close to possible death had her bowels ready to explode. She had been through a lot in her life, but she hadn't been that close to such a gruesome murder, unless one counted watching murder movies on a big screen TV.

There were no cameras inside of the restaurant. She and Geneva, along with five customers and two other kitchen staff where the only ones out of nearly fifty people that night that had not lost their lives.

Geneva lied to the detectives and said she had hidden herself under one of the tables the whole time, which had prevented her from seeing a single face. After she refused to give a statement, the cops gave up on trying any further with her.

Andrea was too afraid to speak to anyone with a badge. She knew who Anthony's guest list was comprised of and she kept on seeing Rubio demanding that she keep her mouth closed. She wasn't dumb at all. The Italian Mafia, no matter in what city, had ties with cops and other forms of the law and the government. Rats were exterminated every day. Period.

The cops left after the restaurant was cleared of all the bodies and body parts. Contractors with the city of Chicago boarded the place up and put yellow tape across the front of it, deeming it still a crime scene.

Andrea put her little denim mini jacket on over her blood-stained uniform shirt and got to walking to get to where she could catch a cab, since it was way past the hours that any CTA buses ran and the three people that normally gave her a ride to the shelter she was staying in were dead.

Tears ran down her face smearing the mascara she had on ran down her face, leaving dark liquid trails from her eyes to her cheeks. Her eyes were red and puffy. She had just gone from only seeing death in the movies to right in front of her own eyes, even wearing it on her face and on her clothes. She knew it was going to be nearly impossible to get any sleep when she got to her bed, at least without downing an entire bottle of something *very* strong.

As she headed along Michigan Avenue towards a well-known taxi pick-up spot, just past the Cheesecake Factory, Andrea heard a horn beep behind her. Her nerves were still in overdrive and she jumped, startled by the horn. She spun around and saw a black Lamborghini truck, on big black custom rims, rolling slowly beside her. Out of fear she started walking faster, thinking Rubio had come back to take her out.

The Urus's horn beeped again. The sound of the driver hitting the gas spooked Andrea. She was about to run for her life, when she heard her name hollered out of the passenger's window. The sound of her name made her finally stop. She turned slowly fearing who it would be when the lights in the SUV turned on and showed her Geneva sitting behind the wheel.

"Hop in," Geneva told her.

Andrea was shocked to see her now former co-worker driving an SUV that she knew was likely at least a half million dollars.

"I'm waitin'," Geneva said, putting the Lambo truck into park, right alongside the curb.

"Who… Who's car is this?" Andrea asked her.

"Mine. Now get in, Andrea. We need to talk."

Andrea took a deep breath, attempting to calm her nerves. She managed to make her feet move. A second later, she was at the passenger's door, opening it up, exposing the black and yellow two-tone interior. She climbed inside, feeling like she had just entered a new dimension of luxury. As soon as she was settled Geneva hit the gas and peeled off.

Andrea was catapulted back into her seat as the twin-turbo V8 engine's magnificent power went to work.

"Um… Geneva… I live at a-" she started to say but then she paused, reluctant to admit to her that she was staying in a shelter for abused women.

"I know where you live, shortie. For now, just ride with me," Geneva told her, crossing over a bridge that ran over the Chicago River.

"But… Geneva-"

"My name is not Geneva," she said, cutting Andrea off, "my name is Monique, but everyone calls me Bunz; *don't* ask why."

Andrea gasped in shock again as Bunz whipped it left onto State Street and headed west towards the E-Way.

"I knew there was something about you, Gene… I mean… Bunz! You got too much ass to be an Asian woman."

Bunz busted out laughing at the white girl.

"But I don't understand. Why are you pretending to be someone else?" she asked Bunz.

Bunz removed the jet black wig and exposed a line on her forehead. Andrea could now see that she was wearing makeup that made her look fair skinned along with golden dreads. Bunz glanced over at her as she cruised onwards, maneuvering through the traffic that was still out and about in the Windy City.

"You'll soon find out. You're with *me* now, 'Drea; no more of that scary-bitch shit. Shit's gon' be on 'n poppin' and

I need someone I know I can trust around me. Am I makin' a mistake by feelin' like that's you?"

"N-No. I'm not a rat and I'm not a snake," Andrea told her as Bunz came to a stop at a red light.

Bunz looked at her and smiled. "Good to know," she replied.

She reached out to the dashboard and pressed the touch screen. She brought up the phone icon and made a call. The sounds of ringing came from the speakers. Andrea stayed quiet while Bunz made her call.

"Yeah?" answered a woman.

"Dumb-dumb 'n 'nem fucked around 'n got sloppy, girl. They gone," Bunz said.

"Wow... all that shit them so-call gangsta niggas was talkin'. So did she...?"

"No. The bitch still breathes. I'm on the way, though."

"Okay. See you when you get here."

Bunz ended the call as the light turned green. She rolled onwards. Andrea sat quietly still, baffled as to what the hell was going on.

Who in the actual fuck is this girl? she thought to herself, glancing over at Bunz, who was looking straight forward, cool, calm, and collected, but inside, she was filled with anger and pure turmoil.

Shooting north on the E-Way, Bunz made her way out to Lake County. The Italian beauty riding next to her was as quiet as a church mouse. Unbeknownst to her, Andrea had been recruited into a world full of getting money, action, drama, and murder. Her heritage alone was the most beneficial aspect of bringing Andrea in but she was more than just an Italian girl to Bunz. She had ways to assist in surefire ways to catch and nail Paula Paulmatti to the cross... *literally.*

A little over an hour later Bunz got to Zion, a small suburban town close to the Illinois-Wisconsin border line. Andrea's eyes stayed open and alert despite how exhausted and fatigued she was. She looked at all the street signs and stores, doing her best to remember where she was going, in case she had to get herself out of there in an emergency.

Close to twenty minutes after hopping off the highway, Bunz made a left turn off Lewis Avenue onto Salem and then immediately turned left into the driveway of a decent-looking 2-story home.

The motion sensor lights around the yard and on the house came on right away. Four muscular Pit Bulls ran out from seemingly nowhere, running right up to the Lambo truck. Andrea saw them and grew nervous as two seemed to stare right at her even with the tinted window rolled up.

"Relax. These are babies compared to what you will see a little later. They won't hurt you either, unless you pose a threat to the owner of this house or anyone associated with her," Bunz told her, killing the engine. "Come on. We're goin' inside for a minute."

Andrea stuck close to Bunz as she led the way to the front door. The dogs, followed, sniffing curiously at Andrea, wondering who the stranger on their property was, but not showing any aggression, since she had arrived with whom they knew, and were comfortable with.

Right as they got to the front door it opened and a 5'6-inch tall woman with cocoa-colored skin and auburn twists opened the door, dressed in a silk robe. She had a sleeping infant in her arms that immediately made Andrea's fear subside. Nobody with a baby that young in their arms could be about to kill a homeless white girl.

With a smile on her face the woman stepped to the side and let Bunz enter, with Andrea behind her. She dismissed the dogs back to guarding the house and closed the door behind her.

Up the stairs, Bunz led the way to the living room, where she introduced Andrea to Tracy. Andrea listened as Bunz filled her in on who Tracy was. It almost brought tears to her eyes and Tracy's when Eric's name was spoken.

"I loved my cousin so much. He made me the woman I am, and he was there for my son like he was his daddy," Tracy wept.

"I'm sorry for your loss, Tracy," Andrea said, "I was adopted; I never met my parents."

Bunz stayed silent as Andrea spoke on how much she wished she could've met the people that brought her into the world. It made her feel bad for a minute, but for what her main mission in life was, there was no room for feelings. She had shit to do, and she needed Andrea for it to happen.

"Where's Nikko at?" Bunz asked Tracy, speaking of Tracy's 16-year-old son.

"I sent him down to his daddy's in Houston for a few weeks. Let his ass deal with that knucklehead for a while."

Bunz chuckled. "I'll be back," she told Tracy and Andrea.

They watched her walk off, then Andrea looked at the baby.

"You have such an adorable baby, Tracy," she told her.

"This little guy isn't mines; he belongs to Monique, and so does his twin sister, who's sleeping in my bed. His name is Eric Jr., and his sister's name is Monique. They're just over a month old."

Tracy leaned down and kissed the tiny little boy's forehead then smiled down at him lovingly. Sitting down on the couch in the luxurious living room, Andrea and Tracy talked for a few minutes then. Andrea started to relax a little more. She didn't feel as out of place as she did just a couple of hours ago.

A few minutes later Andrea saw a woman step into the living room, holding a baby in her arms. She was wearing a brown Fendi shirt and brown leggings with Fendi monogrammed all over them. On her feet she wore brown and beige Fendi sneakers.

She was caramel skinned. Her long gold dreads were hanging loosely down her shoulders, almost to her lower back. When Andrea realized it was Bunz, by her Asian-like face, she gasped.

Holy shit! Bunz is hot! she thought to herself, amazed as the thick and voluptuous beauty headed towards them, with her daughter laughing and giggling at the funny faces and sounds that Bunz was making for her.

"So," Tracy said to Bunz, standing up with Eric Jr. in her arms. "How bad was it exactly?"

"Slaughter; on both sides," Bunz told her, looking up at her. "I knew it would be crazy. Niggas that bump they gums, talkin' all that wannabe gangsta shit, ain't never really on shit."

Tracy shook her head. "Next time, I'll find real goons instead of dumbass block boys."

Tracy had grown up with the man Bunz had pledged her life to. She was Eric's baby sister. They had the same father, but different mothers. Although Tracy was a few years younger than Eric, she was just as tough, just as fearless. He had taught her how to be serious when it came to handling business, and ruthless when it came to bitch ass niggas. She didn't play no games and didn't expect none to be played on her.

"Nevertheless, that little bitch *will* get got sis-in-law," Tracy told Bunz confidently, "she on borrowed time with them connections she got. I put that on my brother's grave."

Bunz nodded her head then looked at Andrea. "We're out. Come on."

Chapter 4

Getting the babies secured in the car seats that Andrea hadn't even noticed were in the rear row, Bunz hopped behind the wheel and made her way north, up to Wisconsin, where she now lived.

When she made it to Caledonia, she hopped off the I-94 and headed east. A few minutes later they entered an upscale neighborhood filled with luxurious homes. The neighborhood was completely secluded. In the back Bunz turned into her freshly seal coated driveway that led up to her mini mansion. Rolling along the curved edge she pulled into a six-car garage and hopped out. Andrea wasn't far behind and proceeded to help her grab the babies out of their car seats.

Andrea's eyes bugged wide open when she saw the biggest dogs that she had ever seen in her life bumble out excitedly, hopping up and down around Bunz. The two-and-a-half-year-old male and female were both dark brown with light brown brindle stripes, clipped ears, and tall, massive muscular bodies. Andrea couldn't believe how big they were. They indeed made the other four dogs at Tracy's house look like Chihuahuas.

"Drea, meet Deuce and LaLa," Bunz said to her, after commanding the 145-pound male, and his 110-pound mate to calm down.

"Why are they so big? What the heck type of pit bulls are they?" Andrea asked, knowing there were some that stayed small, and some that got huge.

"They aren't exactly Pit Bulls; they're XXL Bullies and they like you."

"How do you know that? Andrea asked.

"Because you're still alive. Duh. You have my son in your arms, too. If they felt you had a rotten soul you'd be food already."

She then led Andrea and the dogs into the garage. Inside, Andrea first saw two Rolls-Royce trucks parked next to a yellow Lamborghini Aventador S. Next to the Lambo was a blue Ferrari 488 with red, green, and white racing stripes, and a white convertible Mercedes G650 Maybach truck was next to the 'Rarri.

Andrea was just dumbfounded to constantly discover how rich Bunz was. She was so curious as to what she did for a living. Whatever it was, Andrea wanted in.

***

Bunz carried her son over to where an elevator was built in at one side of the garage. She called it down and stepped in with Andrea, baby Monique, and the dogs. It took them up to the second floor and the doors opened to a luxuriant guest house.

"This is yours until we get you situated," Bunz told her as she led the way into the expansive living room, with a high-end leather couch sectional and a gigantic 4K HDTV screen that was built into the main wall.

Andrea shook her head, finding it all hard to believe. Bunz went to her, gave her a hug, then relieved Andrea of her daughter.

"Make yourself at home. The kitchen is fully stocked, the clothes I have in the bedroom's closet should fit you perfectly, and the bathroom is practically a spa. There's also a brand-new iPhone sitting on the night stand by your bed. My number is already programed into it."

Andrea nodded her head as tears began welling up in her eyes. She blinked them away before they fell down her face. "Bunz?"

Bunz looked at Andrea, peeping how she was trying to maintain her composure.

"Why are you doing this? What's making you bring me into your home? You don't even know me."

"I know enough, Andrea. I was in the same situation as you. I was down; broke, starving, and fuckin' any rich man for a few dollars. Then someone who meant the world helped me, and I did him wrong by ghosting him. By the grace of the Man above, he took me back into his life and made a real woman out of me, despite all the bullshit I came back with," Bunz had to stop her own tears from falling, "I now have the means to be able to help someone else out, so I will. Get some rest and I'll see you in the morning."

Bunz then carried her son and her daughter back to the elevator with the dogs trailing behind her, leaving Andrea to settle in.

***

After she tended to her infant twins, breast-feeding them, burping them, then got them both bathed and in fresh diapers with matching onesies on.

She laid down on the bed next to her little ones and used the iFeeder app she had on her iPhone to electronically fed her dogs via the automatic food and water dispensers in the kitchen. She used the other app on her security list to unlock their dog door so that they could go out when they were ready to use the bathroom.

Lying next to her kids, Bunz waited until Eric Jr. and Monique had fallen asleep, put roll-off blockers around them, and then got up to take a much needed shower.

Her mind was heavy with grief as she stood up. Bunz was so sure that after all those months of laying low to give birth to her children then get herself back in shape, that the recon she had been doing to track down Paula Paulmatti and assembling a team of hungry killers to get her gone, had been enough to avenge her dead fiancé. The images of her shooting Eric, right in front of her, had not left her mind since she had been just four months along in her pregnancy, with their twins.

Eric was the love of Bunz's life. He was a certified gangster, fearless, smart, and ambitious. He was the most incredibly handsome man she had ever met and with a lengthy past of exotic dancing and prostitution, Bunz had met a *lot* of men.

A couple of years ago, she had left him, high and dry, out of nowhere, to chase what she quickly found out was nothing compared to the life she could have had with him, if she had stayed. Bunz had gone on a mission, plotting on a diamond jeweler that was associated with the Italian mob. For two years she had been his bitch in every way, shape, and form. Often, she had been one of his friends' bitches as well, whenever he decided to share her with the other mobsters in his circle that coveted thick beautiful Black women.

Then the night that she had been planning for, for just over 730 days, came. Though Bunz came close to losing her life, the vintage diamond necklace he had in a safe, along with little plastic bags loaded with precious colored diamonds became hers, after she murdered Barry the Diamond man with his own gun she killed one of his security guards and his wife, with that same gun.

She experienced another life-threatening hiccup on the way back to Illinois. Her will to see Eric again allowed her once again to kill to survive and survive she did. Returning to him a couple of days later, unsure if he still lived in the same house, Bunz was accepted back into Eric's life, without too much of a fight. He still loved her and he had not moved on from her.

Bunz had left Eric when he was just a well-off d-boy. When she came back she had discovered that he had elevated his status and was not only just a big dog, but a contract killer and business owner. Immediately, Bunz wanted to learn everything he knew, so that she could be his ride or die chick to the fullest. Everything he did teach her; Bunz took to it like a duckling took to water

Bunz made her way back into the bedroom to make sure the babies hadn't woken up. While in there she looked at where picture frame stands stood on her nightstand. There were quite a few; him by himself, him with his younger play-sister Sonia, and his homeboy Tim, and him with Tracy and her son. There were also a few of Bunz by herself, then quite a few of them together, with LaLa and Deuce. The one she picked up tugged on the strings of her heart the most. It had been taken on the night that Eric had proposed to her. The flawless 8-carat diamond engagement ring he had put on her finger that night, sat inside the little box he had taken it out of. It had been sitting in there since he was killed in front of her. It had been too painful for Bunz to put it on. His smile was too painful to look at. His memory made her heart cry.

Paula Paulmatti had taken her heart. Bunz *vowed* to take *hers* and feed it to her dogs.

* * *

As she stripped out of her clothes to go shower, Bunz heard the little black phone that Eric had always kept with him. She went to the dresser where was tucked away inside of and pulled it out.

The number on the screen was random, as were all the numbers that called that phone, but she pressed answer and put her ear to it.

"I have a problem that I need solved *asap!* Please! Can you help me?!," a woman asked, sounding beyond frantic.

Bunz spoke, using the response that Eric always used when someone contacted him for a job, "Depends."

The woman gave a brief explanation. Bunz immediately accepted the job, feeling the woman's anguish. She told the woman that she would contact her when the job was done and ended the call.

Sighing to herself, Bunz thought about the first job she had received after Eric was killed. She had been handling the business for him through most of her pregnancy, with help from Tracy and another one of Eric's young associates that had become like a little brother to her, because she was dead set on keeping Eric's legacy alive.

Finally getting up, Bunz headed back to the shower. She entered the custom-designed spa-style master bathroom and went to the walk-in glass shower. Turning the hot water on full blast, she let it pour down on her from the custom *Rain Down* style ceiling directly above her.

As she let the water pelt her skin, Bunz thought about Andrea, and everything she knew about the 23-year-old. She didn't know it yet, but Andrea was the biggest part of Bunz's ultimate plan

***

"Monique. Baby. I can't even describe the ways that I love you. You truly complete me, my queen."

"Aww! E, you're gonna make me cry! I'm pregnant, man!" she chuckled as her eyes began welling up with tears from his passionate words.

"Naw, baby. Don't cry; this is a night for smiles and happiness," Eric told her.

He then dug into his pocket and pulled out a little cream-colored velvet box.

Bunz's eyes went wide, then, as Eric sank down to one knee, she screamed so loud that everyone in the restaurant looked their way to see what happened.

He opened the box and revealed the flawless 8-carat diamond engagement ring inside. Bunz gasped when she saw it.

"Monique Reese Duque...will you make me the happiest man on earth, more than I already am, and marry me?"

"Yes!" she exclaimed, "Yes! Yes! Yesss!"

***

Bunz's eyes shot open as the dream jolted her out of her sleep. She shot up in her bed, shaking and trembling. She looked around and saw that she was in her new bedroom, not the one she had shared with Eric. Tears welled up in her eyes. She just could not believe that he was really gone. It hurt her so bad.

I swear to fucking God! When I catch that bitch I'ma peel her skin from off her body while the bitch is still alive! Bunz thought to herself, seething with anger for Paula Paulmatti.

She laid back down and closed her eyes, but for the rest of the night, she could not get back to sleep.

***

The next morning, still fatigued from the night before, Bunz managed to get herself out of bed and tend to her babies. After she breastfed Eric Jr. and Monique she cooked breakfast which consisted of scrambled eggs and bacon, for herself and the dogs. She went and got in the shower and got herself dressed in a chocolate-colored Fendi outfit, consisting of a leather mini-jacket with the designer name monogrammed all over it, a black low-cleavage shirt with *Fendi* in chocolate-brown letters across the bosom, and skin-tight monogrammed leather leggings that accentuated her shapely bottom half and made her fat juicy ass look like it was made of chocolate.

On her feet, she put on glossy chocolate-colored 6-inch pointed-toe pumps that elongated her toned legs. After she applied a little makeup from her Fenty makeup kit, put her dreads up in ball on the top of her head, and gelled her baby hair edges down, she put her big yellow-gold hoop earrings in her ears, two long yellow-gold chains around her neck, and her custom-made Fendi watch that had yellow diamonds embedded into the gold bezel. She looked at herself in the tall full-body mirror that took selfies when the voice recognition heard her saw '*SNAP!*' Lastly, she spritzed on some Rihanna perfume, grabbed her Fendi shades, then got her babies into the carry seats and took them out to the garage with the dogs following.

***

Andrea smiled when she saw how good she looked in the mirror. She loved what she saw. After showering, she chose a sexy green leather Saint Laurent by Anthony Vacarello dress that had gold studs embedded on the shoulders and around the mid-section, with a slit going up the left leg from the above-the-knee hem.

With the brand new LaPerla bra and thong set, she had an enticing pair of nude fishnet pantyhose set out to go with the form-fitting dress.

Now that she was dressed she applied a little makeup to her beautiful face, put her hair up in a high ponytail and flossed out in the gold jewelry that Bunz had there for her. When she was done, she slid her feet into metallic gold Saint Laurent 6" pumps.

"Wow," Andrea said, turning her 5'6" tall frame to the side and marveling at how plump her 37-inch ass looked from how tight and shiny the dress was, and how much more bigger it made her 32-C cup breasts look from the low cleavage line. She felt like a somebody; she felt good. Like she was finally somewhat relevant.

***

Andrea disconnected her new iPhone from off the charger and called Bunz. She was told to come down into the garage.

Grabbing the green diamond-stitched YSL handbag that had also been set out for her, Andrea headed out of her guest house to the elevator. When it reached the main floor of the garage, she saw the door to the port where the ruby-red Rolls-Royce Cullinan sat was opened. Bunz was sitting in the passenger's seat, looking her way.

Andrea walked up to the passenger's window and looked at Bunz, looking like a celebrity in the SUV's white and ruby-red accented wood grain interior.

"I hope you can drive; this is not a cheap truck," Bunz told her, hitting the unlock button, prompting Andrea to get behind the wheel.

Andrea went and got in. She saw that behind her Eric Jr. and Monique were secured in their baby seats while the dogs sat side by side on the ruby-red carpeted floor.

"Um… I don't have a license, Bunz," Andrea told her.

Bunz shrugged. "Neither did I at first. Take us down to Tracy's crib. I need to drop my babies off. We have some runs to make and we can't have babies with us."

Andrea nodded her head, then she looked at the dashboard and the steering wheel.

"Uh… where's the…?"

Bunz reached over and hit the push-start button. The twin-turbo V12 engine fire right up and purred like a kitten out of the exhaust pipes.

"Okay, um, now the…?" Andrea said, looking for how to put it in drive.

Bunz chuckled. "Not exactly a BMW, huh?" she joked, reaching over to point out the little column shifter.

Andrea, embarrassed that she hadn't ever been in a vehicle worth more than $5,000 in her life, put it in reverse and backed out of the garage.

"I need a job, Bunz," she said, putting it in drive when she was out of the garage and pulling off to head down the driveway.

"You're hired," Bunz told her.

"Huh?" Andrea glanced over at her, approaching the road.

"You work for me now, shortie."

"Okay… but doing what?"

"Solving problems for people. You'll see," Bunz said, as Andrea turned out and made a left onto 4 Mile.

Deciding it was best to find out instead of playing 21 questions Andrea just leaned back in the seat and cruised her way to I-94, to head south to Zion and drop the kids off so she and Bunz could do whatever it was that Bunz had plans for.

Chapter 5

Andrea and Bunz made their way to Tracy's where they dropped off the twins. After kissing her babies goodbye Tracy handed Bunz a plain black briefcase. Andrea watched the exchange growing more and more curious with each passing second. Even with curiosity eating her alive she managed to not ask. She was sure that when the time came, she would know. And if it never came then it wasn't her business.

Briefcase in hand Bunz led Andrea back to the car and hopped in. As they pulled out, Deuce and LaLa were laid out of the soft carpet, enjoying the luxuriously soft ride as Andrea made her way down Route 173, back towards 94.

Bunz's iPhone began beeping just then. She pulled it out of her monogrammed Fendi bag and saw the alert that had popped up on the custom-designed app that only she and Eric had. Immediately, Bunz reached out to turn down Drake's *Unforgettable* featuring Young Jeezy as it bumped from the stock audio system.

"Change of plans," she told Andrea, urgently, seeing the little red dot on the GPS was very close to their current location. "When we get to Route 41 make a left and *floor it!*"

Andrea could tell that Bunz was dead-ass serious. When she got to the 173 and 41 intersection she hooked a hard left, just making it through the yellow light. She floored it, blazing by a line of semi-trucks and a few cars.

Bunz opened the suitcase that Tracy had given her as Andrea passed by another semi. Andrea glanced over, catching sight of the briefcase being opened in her peripheral view. She saw Bunz pull out a shiny black semi-automatic 9-millimeter pistol from the insert inside the foam holder. Bunz took a silencer out of another insert, screwed it into the barrel, then grabbing a loaded clip, she slapped it in and cocked it, chambering a round.

Oh shit! Oh shit! What the hell is happening? Andrea thought to herself, getting nervous as she rounded a curve in the road that led her to another straight shot with a big intersection a quarter mile up.

"Relax, 'Drea," Bunz told her, as she rested her Sig Sauer on her lap, "we're about to solve our first problem together; do what I tell you, and it'll be like ridin' a bike."

***

Ramon sat in his 2022 Audi A8, choking his ass off after he took a puff of the Granddaddy Purp' he had just sparked up. As the Garcia Vega burned slowly water poured down over his car from the automatic car wash he was inside of.

On the seat next to him was a backpack full of cash. In the back, sitting on the rear seat, an expensive merle-colored French Bulldog that he had snatched from his ex-girlfriend, who he had also stolen the bag of money from.

He had been dating the wealthy girl for a while. She was head over hills in love with him and did anything for him but, the whole time, Ramon had been using her for his own personal gain. He didn't give a shit about her, only her money.

He'd drained her bank accounts, tricked her into helping him build his credit up by destroying her own; he even managed to make her fuck and suck all his friends, telling her that a good chick did any and everything her man told her to do, without backtalking him. The Audi he was pushing, he had suckered the girl into getting for him off her credit, promising to make the payments, then abruptly switching up on her, leaving her owe the remaining $47,500 to pay off on her own. She was as gullible as a young kid trying to prove himself to older thrill-seekers and he had taken full advantage of her until, one day, she got wise and attempted to boot him.

The Bulldog barked and growled at Ramon.

"Shut cho' lil' bitch ass up before I sell yo' ass to someone that's into bestiality," he told the angry canine.

Turning his head back to the windshield, Ramon turned the music up and toked on his loud as Yo Gotti bumped, pounding from the woofers in the trunk as the auto wash slowly rolled him to the next section of the carwash.

Globs of soapy foam started spraying all over it, then the brushes came. After the final rinse, the powerful dryers blew the car dry. High as a kite, Ramon took a deep breath to get ready to drive again. He saw the exit door rolling up. He put his car in drive and was heading to leave out, when out of nowhere, the rear end of a dark-red Rolls-Royce truck backed up and blocked him inside.

"Maaaan, what the fuck, joe?" Ramon beeped the horned and yelled at the driver. The Frenchie barked at him again. *"Shut the fuck up!"*

TAP TAP TAP

Hearing tapping on the window, he turned his head to the left and found himself staring into the barrel of a pistol with a silencer. It was held by a beautiful woman, in a sexy brown Fendi outfit.

"Get out, or *die*," he heard her say from the other side of the glass.

"Hold up, shortie! Don't shoot, aight!" Ramon freaked, raising his hands up.

"Then get *out*, dick head."

Ramon hit the unlock button and cautiously got out of the car. The woman was taller than him. She was so thick that even with a gun pointed at his face he still couldn't help but glance down at her hips and thighs.

"Step back," she told him, gesturing him to the side with the barrel.

"What is this, man?" Ramon asked, hands still up, stepping to his left, "Do I know you?"

"No, you don't," the girl said, making him keep on stepping back until he was under the soap sprayers, "but I know *you*, you lil' punk bitch scam artist."

Ramon gasped. "Naw! Aye, she's lyin' to-"

The girl fired a round at the computer just outside of where the main sprayer was. The machine malfunctioned and started spraying. In seconds, Ramon was covered in hot foam, blinding him. The soap started burning his eyes. He cursed and hollered in pain, falling to his knees, trying to rub the soap out of his eyes.

PFFT! PFFT! PFFT! PFFT! PFFT! PFFT!

Bunz popped his ass repeatedly, even after he was face down and leaking out onto the soapy ground. She emptied the thirteen rounds in her clip in his face, chest, then his back Dead and bleeding out, Ramon turned the foam he was covered in red like cherry Kool-Aid.

After she had put the last bullet in the back of his head Bunz hurried to the Audi and got behind the wheel, closing the door. The French Bulldog in the back seat barked at her. She turned around and smiled at him.

"Hiiii, cutie pie!" She patted her lap, calling him to her. He jumped from the back seat to her, then started hopping around on her lap, excited to be around someone with a good soul. "Aww! You're so sweet! Let's take you back to your mommy! She misses you *sooooo* much," Bunz told him then kissed his nose.

***

Andrea's jaw hung agape when she saw how fast and easy she had just laid the guy down. She watched Bunz hop into his car then ten seconds later she was pulling forward, leaving the guy in the fluffy red foam, beeping at her to go.

Pulling up, Andrea let Bunz get around her, then she followed her around the side of the gas station. Not a single person that was fueling up or inside making purchases looked in their direction.

Holy shit! Wow! I can't believe it! Bunz is a killer, Andrea thought to herself, as she followed Bunz out onto the highway and hit it to keep up with her. She then thought to herself, *I need to learn everything she knows so, one day, I can get that sick bastard back for everything he did to me…*

Bunz about-faced and led Andrea north. She took the Audi, the dog, and the bag of cash out to Beloit, Wisconsin. The young freckle-faced white girl was waiting for her outside of her luxurious log-cabin styled mansion. Overjoyed to have her dog back, the girl squealed when she got him in her arms. She was so happy that she decided to let Bunz keep the backpack full of money even though she had already paid her. She had found Bunz through her dealer after explaining the situation that her piece of shit ex had left her in.

After patting the bulldog's head Bunz made her way back to the vehicle that Andrea was driving. She tossed her backpack and told her to open it.

"Whoa!" Andrea gasped when she saw all the $20s, $50s, and $100s, all rubber-banded up. "That's, damn, this is a lot of money, Bunz!"

"Eh," Bunz shrugged, "it's enough to pay some bills for a few years, but it's nothin' compared to the money that will come in for the big jobs. By the way, that's yours to keep. You just made your first paycheck at your new part-time job! Congratulations, girl!"

Shaking her head, Andrea couldn't help but smile. She sighed to herself, looking at the money once more. She realized then that she was in the prime position to boss up.

"Thank you, Bunz. For real. This... this means a lot to me."

Bunz nodded her head. "You earned it; just for the record, nobody we kill will be a saint. That guy took advantage of that girl so fuck him. Now let's roll, shortie. I have another stop I need to make and I'm hungry as hell too, like I know you are."

Andrea put her money in the backseat with LaLa and Deuce then pulled off, heading in the direction that Bunz told her to go.

***

After meeting the client Bunz spoke to earlier on the phone at a Denny's out in Gurnee, Andrea felt such rage burning inside of her that she never thought she would be capable of feeling.

Bunz was beyond infuriated.

"Let's go," she told Andrea, pulling a $50 from her wallet and dropping it on the table.

Andrea got up, leaving the woman and her tear-filled eyes at the table. Following Bunz out, she attempted to stop her own tears from falling. The job the woman called upon Bunz for had seriously touched their hearts. They were both seething that people were so evil to other people. They were both *dying* to handle this one.

Chapter 6

"Yeah, man, I'm tryna' tell you, homie! I got hoes, I got money, and I got drugs all through this muhfucka! On Crip! Niggas tryna get high, they come see *me*! Niggas tryna' get some pussy, they come slide on Big Crippin' and I tell one of these hoes to gon' ahead and gi' 'dat pussy up. But 'ya gots to pay first, 'ya feel me?"

The young gullible 23-year-old white boy nodded his head. His eyes were lit up as if the older inmate had just handed him the gift of eternal life, with a bad bitch on the side.

"Fa' sho, man! What they call you, bro?" the boy asked the husky brown-skinned dread-head, with a thick beard that was infused with gray hairs.

"They call me the King around here, lil' bruh."

"Okay. Cool, dude. I'm Justin."

King shook the white boy's hand then dismissed him. He watched Justin leave out of the bathroom, then he crept over to the bathroom toilet stall. He tapped on it lightly and waited.

The door opened and inside, King saw the transgender inmate standing on top of the toilet, trying to hide still. When the white boy had barged in, urgently needing to take a piss, King and his secret transgender lover had to abruptly stop what they were doing in the stall.

As a prisoner in the Sturtevant Correctional Center, out in Racine, Wisconsin, King portrayed himself as the man to see if one needed illicit drugs and claimed to have females staff members that would fuck and suck for the right price, once the cash hit *his* hands. While he claimed this, not even one of the many different factions of mobs that inhabited the prison honored him. King only had been able to get the business of the dumb ones that had just came from the classification prison out in Waupun, Wisconsin. Once they found out that the man that claimed to be a Crip from California was fucking multiple transgender inmates, thinking he was on the low, and snitching, King lost business and respect. Nobody knew how he was still walking around so freely but many knew that soon he wouldn't be.

To make matters worse, he was locked up for molesting his own brother's daughter then he shot and killed his brother when the man came at him to seek revenge. There were so many death threats on King but everyone was scared to touch him, knowing what he would do.

"Can we finish, big daddy? the tranny asked, nearly begging for King to come back into the stall.

King looked at the white transgender woman. He had seen ones that looked like women in the 25 years he had been gone. He wanted to curl his lip up with disgust; he only started messing with this one, because it had been easy to get what he wanted out of the individual.

"Naw. I gotta make some moves. I'll see you later, aight, Pam?" King said, calling him by the name "she" preferred to be called.

Frustration flashed in the trans inmate's eyes. King ignored it and left out of the bathroom before he got caught in the bathroom with a man wearing makeup, panties, and rolled-up socks inside of a bra.

King hurried out of the multipurpose building and headed towards his unit. As he strolled down the walk, a whole lot of inmates that were in the courtyards of the other units surrounding the center basketball courts and weight piles, stopped what they were doing, and looked at the known tranny-pimp walking as if he was God.

King paid them no attention. He headed to his unit, ignoring the shouts and threats that came from the gangsters, hustlers, and even plain inmates that just hated snitches and snakes.

It was a hot summer day. All King had on his mind was getting changed out of his greens and into his sweats so he could go for a run around the track then shower and hop on the phone to call his woman, whom had no clue that he was fucking trannies in prison.

He entered the housing unit he was in and, again, had so many eyes that were filled with malice and hatred on him. It made him smile to himself. He loved it when people hated on him for doing what he did. Even those *real* goons. He relished in the fact that nobody could touch him, because he would press charges on them, like he had done before when he got his ass beat the fuck up.

After he changed into his new sweat suit and put on his running shoes, King went back outside and ran just half a lap, before he was out of breath, and sweating like a nervous pig. He walked the rest of the way back to where he had started.

"Aye King! What up baby!"

King turned and saw Grimey G hurrying towards him. King clenched his teeth when he saw the fat, dark-skinned clown huffing and puffing as he tried to make his 340-pound body go faster than a snail.

Grimey G was one of the barbers at the prison and did hair on the units. Nobody knew exactly how that was possible since he only had one *real* eye. He was a gossip girl to the core and a straight up pervert. The man religiously tried to get at every female staff member he saw that looked at him, thinking they wanted him just because they attempted to be nice and respectful by saying hi when he said hello to him. He had no clue that they all despised his fat, nasty, clown ass with a passion, especially because he had a big afro with a big bald spot up on top of the back of his head.

"Aye, my nigga! What's happenin', baby?" Grimey G asked, dapping King up.

"The money you owe me is what's up, fam," King told him, continuing to walk with Grimey G at his side, "When I'ma see that?"

"Aww, man. See, what happen was, my baby momma ain't get paid, man, and the bitch claim my son needed some diapers 'n shit. So, I gotta wait. It's all good, baby! I got chu'!"

King cast a side glance at him. "You been locked up how long?"

"5 years. Why you ask that?" Grimey G questioned.

"You girl has a baby that's in diapers... that is not yo' child, G."

"Yeah, it is. I was plugged when I was in the other joint, before I came here," Grimey G capped, as they rounded a turn at the bottom of the track that led alongside an inner road where a barbwire fence was. "I had staff lettin' me take my bitch in the visitin' bathroom so I could fuck her. I got her pregnant, fam."

Naw, nigga, one of them COs fucked yo' bitch in the parkin' lot and he *the daddy, dumbass nigga*, King thought to himself, chuckling to himself.

"I hear you, my nigga. That's what's up," he said instead.

Just then, a van being driven by a female correctional officer on ride-around duty for the shift was rolling past on the road outside of the fence. Grimey G saw her and immediately started shouting out to her.

"Aayyee, Ms. Cervantes! You looking good today, girl, can I ride with you?"

The woman didn't even so much as turn her head to look his way. King busted out laughing as Grimey G's face fell to the ground.

"Nigga, these bitches don't want no fat-ass nigga that don't got no money, nor do they want a nigga with an afro that got a big-ass bald spot on the top of his head that look like a bird been layin' on it," King said.

And these niggas gon' kill yo' gay snitchin' ass, bitch ass nigga, Grimey G thought to himself, salty as hell that he couldn't bump a bitch and was steadily being teased about it his bald spot.

PFFT!

Suddenly, King's head exploded, right when he was about to speak again. Blood and brains flew all over Grimey G.

"Oh shiiit? What the-"

PFFT!

"Aaaagggghhh!" Grimey G screamed as pain exploded in his ass.

A silenced bullet slammed into his ass and completely obliterated it, much like the one that had blown King's head off.

The inmates on the yard that heard Grimey G's scream all looked down to where they were and saw the bloody scene. A few gasped in shock while others all looked with either amazement or laughed their asses off.

CO's and sergeants came running from different housing units when the CO in the gun tower that was closest to the scene rang the alarm over the radio.

Grimey G continued screaming in agony until another bullet came flying, smacking right into the bald spot in the back of his afro, taking his whole head off. His headless corpse fell right down next to King's, and they both bled out onto the track.

***

Andrea laughed her ass off as she ran behind Bunz. Together they dipped off from the huge mound behind the prison that allowed for the perfect perch for a sniper to pop an inmate and get up out of there. Running with LaLa and Deuce on their trail, the two ladies made a clean getaway from the prison's perimeter.

"Holy shit, Bunz! You blew those motherfuckers' heads off!" Andrea exclaimed as they jumped into Bunz's Cullinan.

Bunz set the Barrett .50 caliber sniper rifle to the side and peeled off from the spot in the woods where she'd had Andrea park. She hurried down the dirt road and hopped back onto the street, heading north.

"Creeps and wannabe gangsters deserve to die," Bunz told Andrea, despising them with everything in her, "Especially the under-cover homos that my report told me the one with the dreadlocks was."

Andrea shook her head. "I be hearin' about those in-the-closet guys in prison; they think what they do in there won't follow them to the street, and I hear too how motherfuckers that be in prison snitching 'n shit, think it's cool 'til a CO puts their asses on blast. Then they gotta go to sleep *knowin'* they're a rat."

Bunz chuckled.

"But why'd you shoot the fat dude? Andrea then asked, as Bunz decreased her speed down to the speed limit.

Bunz laughed again. "I could tell he talked too damn much and that bald-spot was getting' on my nerves."

Andrea howled out laughing at her. A few minutes later, Bunz came to a stop sign. With no cars coming up behind her, she quickly pulled out her phone and typed a fast text. *Problem solved; no charge*, she told the client that had sought her out to get King, who had happened to be the mother of the little girl he had molested.

Rolling off again, Bunz hit a left turn and headed west. She had another stop to make and Andrea needed to see *that* side of her business as well.

Chapter 7

Bunz drove out to Kenosha. She turned into the parking lot of a small plaza that had a beauty salon, a pet store, a popular little soul food restaurant and, as a new addition, a top-of-the line clothing boutique that had been built onto the corner of the business block, right off Green Bay and Washington Road.

Besides the clothing store, which Bunz had built with her own money, the plaza was created by Eric. In his passing Bunz assumed ownership of it as well, seeking to keep everything he had built from hard work alive and well. She had plans to add more soon. She wanted everyone to know that even though he was gone, his name was still relevant, and anybody that doubted it, she was going to see them.

She went around the front of it, riding slow through the packed parking lot. Andrea saw a lot of women inside of the salon, laughing at whatever was being talked about while getting their hair and nails done. Rounding the last building, Bunz went behind the buildings, to where the back of the salon was.

Andrea saw the white Porsche 911 Turbo S parked behind a green Tesla Model S. Bunz parked behind the Tesla and killed the engine. She grabbed the sniper rifle and opened her door to get out with the dogs jumping out behind her, telling Andrea to hop out and follow.

Bunz entered the code into the electronic pad lock, then put her right eye to the retina scanner at the side of the. A second later, the high-strength steel door unlocked. Bunz led them all inside and closed the door. Andrea saw racks of high-end designer clothing, shoes, and accessories for women and men all over the room. Wowed by it all, Andrea felt like she had just walked into the most exclusive designer store ever.

Bunz took the big sniper rifle to where a rack with Gucci swag was. She moved it aside and behind it, was a little metal door. She slid it up and opened the thick steel door that was behind it. Putting the Barrett inside, she closed both doors as quickly as she had opened them.

Andrea came over was she pressed a button on the side of it and a second later, the sounds of whooshing came from inside.

"Never keep a dirty gun," Bunz told Andrea, as the hide-away incinerator melted the sniper rifle down inside, reducing it into a puddle. "You will *always* get caught with it."

Andrea nodded her head in understanding then followed Bunz through another door that led out to the main floor of the shopping area. Andrea was wowed by all the expensive swag that littered the boutique. Everything someone could want if they had money in their pocket was available for purchase.

"Get what you want," Bunz then told her, "Go crazy; there's no limit."

Surprised, but reassured when Bunz nodded her head to reconfirm that she had heard her right, Andrea wasted no time in going to look at all the top-brand designer labels.

Bunz informed the manager of the store that if Andrea needed help, to make it happen. The woman nodded her head then Bunz headed out to head over to the beauty salon, needing to check on a different type of inventory.

***

In the basement of the salon, specially built by her would-have-been husband, Bunz entered the lit-up space to find the group of beautiful naked ladies all working hard. Some were breaking down kilos of raw cocaine and mixing them up for snorters, while others were cooking up crack; there were four ladies mixing up raw heroin, stretching it all the way out, then the others were sorting various kinds of opioid pills or counting the cash that had just come in with money counters.

LaLa and Deuce stayed right by her side as greetings from the ladies all poured in. Though it had been half a year past when Eric was shot the ladies, that had worked for him prior to Bunz taking over and keeping his businesses running, were still grieving. To them, the loss was so great, that all of them felt like their hearts had been taken straight out of their chests and stepped on.

For many of them, until Eric had entered their lives, and offered multiple ways to get their bucks up, they were on the streets, hurting and twerking for dollars instead of checking big bags of money every week, like they were doing now.

They handled drugs and money and because of how hard they worked, they they all were pushing a new foreign whip, lived lavishly, and had long money, thanks to Eric putting them on and never taking advantage of them.

Bunz looked at the stash of cocaine and saw how low they were. She looked over at the table with wrapped bales of money and knew it was time for the re-up. She pulled out her phone and went in to her contacts, finding *Bro* in seconds.

I think it's about time for us to have dinner, bro. I'm in the mood for a big meal. Are you free any time soon? she texted, then she put her phone back in her handbag and headed over to speak with the poison-green Mohawk wearing chick that was in charge of the underground operation.

***

Andrea gasped when she saw *him* enter the store, carrying a leather Gucci book bag. He was tall, light-skinned, sported a fresh bald-fade haircut with a razor-sharp beard lining. As he came further into the store, heading for the check-out counter, looking so fresh and clean in an Amiri fit with the feet-bone high-top Amiri sneakers on his feet, Andrea saw that his eyes were the color of a cloud free summertime sky. Andrea swore he had a strong resemblance to Steph Curry but he was *waaay* bulkier than the Golden State Warrior star.

Wow! He is so hot! Who is he? she wondered to herself, still holding the leather Balmain Paris dress that she wanted to try on.

"We all think the same thing that you're thinking inside of your head right now, 'Drea," said Kylie, a thick redbone that was the store's manager, interrupting Andrea's lusty thoughts.

Andrea still couldn't take her eyes off the guy. He set the book bag up on the check-out counter, giving the cashier a smile as she took the bag, smiling herself like a love-struck girl in high school.

"Is he her boyfriend?" Andrea asked Kylie, as four other girls nearly fought over who was going to stand next to him at the counter.

"Lookin' that fine, you would think he had a hundred girlfriends, but no. He isn't in a relationship with anyone, especially in this store," Kylie told her, looking at him with longing eyes of her own, "He's good friends with Bunz, kind of like a little brother to her, but he was Eric's homeboy, too. He was living out of town until Eric… passed. He came to help Bunz out with business and the kids."

Andrea heard the guy laugh when the girls started trying to push up on him. He gave them all hugs then. Andrea smiled at that. He seemed to be a nice guy, but she wondered what he was like in a more private way.

"You wanna' try that one on?" Kylie asked, interrupting Andrea again.

"Um…. yeah, yes," Andrea said, nearly tripping over herself as she gazed at him.

Just then, he looked her way. Andrea gasped; embarrassed that she had just gotten caught staring. But when he smiled and gave her a head nod she smiled back, feeling like a little girl that had just met her favorite celebrity.

"Come on, little Paris Hilton, before you open up a box that might contain a surprise that's way too big for you," Kylie said to her.

With the four other dresses and skirts on hangers, Kylie took the Balmain dress and ushered Andrea towards the fitting rooms.

***

Bunz and Tanzania laughed their asses off as they watched Andrea, and the other girls as usual, gush over Tim when he walked in. Watching from the security camera app on her iPhone.

"How did I know that she was gon' get hit with Cupid's arrow when Timbo came in?" Bunz asked herself.

"Because that blue-eyed nigga is *fiiiiiiiiiine*!" exclaimed Bunz's basement bottom bitch. "I just can't believe that he ain't fucked every chick that works in this plaza yet, especially all the ones that throw him the pussy every chance they get."

"Like *you* do?" Bunz replied, with a sly smile, as she turned and looked at the 5'6" tall honey-mustard complexioned chick.

Tanzanian started smiling her ass off, then standing in her Red Bottom pumps that matched her mohawk, turned and grabbed a hold of her desk and started making her fat juicy ass clap.

"A bitch like me wants what I want, and a nigga like that wants ass like this fat juicy muthafucka speakin' to you right now," she told Bunz. She stopped and turned as Bunz laughed her ass off. "This pussy gon' be all up in Timmy Tim Tim's face one day, *baayybeee*!"

Bunz shook her head, still laughing her ass off at the freaky green head that did not hide how much she loved sex. She was about to speak when her phone buzzed in her bag. She pulled it out and saw a reply from Macho.

Yep. See you tomorrow, lil' sis, he had told her.

Cool. Thanks, big bro, Bunz replied.

"Macho will see us tomorrow," Bunz told Tanzania.

"Mmmmm mmmm *mmmm*! Now *that* nigga is *too* damn handsome! I will fuck him anywhere he wants it, girl," Tanzania stated, with starry eyes.

"I will tell you now; if you ever let his wife or his girlfriend hear you say that I will not be able to help you when you get chopped up into bite-size pieces and stuffed into some fruit cans."

Tanzania's smile immediately fell. "Well, that's graphic."

The little black business phone rang right then. Bunz pulled it out and answered it.

"Speak on it," she said, then she heard the nasally voice of a man.

"I have a problem that *really* needs to be solved! Like *today*! Can you *pleeeaase* help me?" he begged, sounding like he had a life and death situation.

Bunz's eyebrows furrowed up. She was going to have to narrow down ways that people got the business phone number.

"Depends," she said.

The guy explained what he deemed to be an emergency. Bunz shook her head. It took everything in her to keep herself from laughing.

"Okay, then. Send me the location, asap, and I'll contact you as soon as your... problem, is solved, sir."

She ended the call and looked at Tanzania.

"This is a very strange world, girl."

Tanzania chuckled. "You're tellin' me. Where else does a punk-bitch wannabe president get shot in his ear then a week later, when the bandage comes off... ain't no scars, no scratches...nothin'! And his bitch ass finna lose to a muthafuckin' Sistah!"

"*Finally!*" Bunz exclaimed, dapping up the green headed woman and rapping her version of Young Jeezy's *My President.*

"Again, my president will be black and a female. Women run this world, yeah bitch, we will prevail!"

Tanzania laughed her ass off at Bunz. "*Heeeeell* naw! This bitch is cray-cray, joe!"

***

Kylie's moth hung agape as did Cynthia's, Amerie's, Deidra's, Sylvie's, and Asia's, as they all watched Tim put his phone number into Andrea's iPhone.

"That shit is *crazy*," Asia said, jealous as hell of the white girl getting the handsome-ass Black man that they all wanted.

"It's always a white bitch that takes the handsome brothers that aren't assholes," Deidra added, shaking her head.

Cynthia, Amerie, and Sylvie were dumbfounded. Kylie was shocked but happy for the girl. Bunz had filled her in on Andrea's life. In *her* opinion, Andrea deserved some good things to come into her life. If it started with a job, making big bank, true friendship, and came with a good man, then Kylie supported it.

"That bitch ain't even all that," Amerie hated, looking the Italian beauty up and down, with a curled upper lip.

"Nope," said Cynthia, with a hand on her hip.

"I'll beat that soft-ass bitch up, joe," said Sylvie, pissed beyond belief, because Tim had never even so much as ever even looked at her, much less gave her the million-dollar smile that he was giving Andrea.

"Sounds to *me* like y'all need to step y'all's game up."

The girls jumped when they heard Bunz's voice behind them. They all turned and saw the boss there, holding two heavy duffel bags, with her two big dogs, both of whom were known to have no problem eating whoever Bunz commanded them to eat.

Sylvie started stammering in fear of the look on Bunz's face. "Bunz! Um… we were just… um…"

"Hating on a girl who has had a really rough life and *still* is able to attract the attention of a man you *all* pine for?"

Not a single one of them answered.

"Let me make this really clear right now to all of you," Bunz said, giving all of them some eye contact. "People *die* for *less* than what you bitches are doin'. Knock it the fuck off, *now*."

"Sorry," they all said in unison.

"Bunz!"

She turned to see an excited Andrea coming towards her. Following behind was Tim, with a big smile on his face.

Andrea thanked her graciously for all the new swag and accessories, hugging her emphatically.

"Whaz' good, family?" Tim then said to Bunz, giving her a brotherly hug.

"Same ol' thang, playboy. I see you met my home girl 'Drea," Bunz said, then narrowing her eyes at him, she added, "Don't pull that pretty boy Ginuwine shit on her, Timmy, or my foot's goin' up yo' ass."

Tim raised his hands in surrender, chuckling to himself, while Andrea started blushing.

"I ain't on that, sis. Lil' mama seems like a classy lady. I wanna' get to know her a little better is all."

The other girls stayed where they were, being super nebby.

55

"Um, Bunz," Andrea spoke. "We should go out, 'ya know? Like, to celebrate my new... job."

Bunz laughed. "That sounds like a good idea, for a woman that doesn't have to infant twins." She looked at Tim. "Why don't *you* two go out and have some fun?"

"I'm down," Tim said, smiling at Andrea, making her feel like she had butterflies in her stomach.

Andrea cheesed her ass off back at him, legs crossed under her, attempting to stop the thumping feeling between her legs and the moisture that she could feel wetting her thong.

Bunz saw the *wet-pussy* face that Andrea had. "Down girl," she told her, patting Andrea's head. "Help me take these bags to the car, please. Tim. She'll be ready around 10:00 p.m. sharp. Don't be late, dude."

Tim nodded his head. "I wouldn't dare," he said, and gave Andrea a flirtatious wink.

Chapter 8

"What the hell?" Andrea furrowed when she saw the Rolls-Royce truck was gone. In its place was a glossy burgundy-pearl colored Bentley Bentayga, siting up on big Forgiatos that were chromed with burgundy accents. "Where's…the other truck?"

Bunz chuckled as she hit the button on the key fob remote, starting the twin-turbo 12-cylinder engine under the hood.

"Gots to change the paint, lil' mama," Bunz told her, remembering one of the first lessons Eric taught her, on the first day she had solved problems with him.

She took one of the bags to the rear of the Bentley truck and lifted the back hatch. Andrea, LaLa, and Deuce followed. Bunz opened the door, revealing that the exclusive interior matched the exterior paint, with Bentley luggage stacked on one side. At the opposite side, Bunz reached in and pressed on a spot that was just over the right rear wheel. A trap door flipped open then. She put the bag inside and closed it back.

"The other bag is ridin' with us," she told Andrea, closing the hatch back down.

They hopped into the Bentley truck and headed off. Bunz shot out to a Wal-Mart up in Racine, on Duran Road and parked. Andrea leaned back in her seat, listening to the newest song by Doja Cat while the dogs sat on the rear seats, looking out of the windows.

Five minutes after parking, Bunz saw the vehicle she was waiting for pulling up. Andrea saw the shiny dark-gray Mercedes S600 coupe pull up on chromed AMG rims. The windows were so darkly tinted that she couldn't see who was inside.

The driver parked the 2-door Benzo next to Bunz's Bentayga and killed the engine. Andrea then saw a petite Asian woman with fair-skin and brown hair pulled back into a bun, get out. She was wearing a light brown correctional officer's shirt, tucked into dark brown uniform pants, with black Timberlands on her feet. On the sleeves of her short-sleeved shirt, the lady had three yellow upward-pointing arrows, indicating her rank.

The lady saw Deuce in the rear driver's side window and lit up with excitement. She rushed to the back door, opening it and cooing over him. Andrea saw how excited he and LaLa got at the woman's presence.

"Damn, boy! You are too damn big, now!" the woman said, sounding like a hood chick as Deuce's tail went crazy, smacking the lady's side, "and you, too, LaLa!"

"What up, Jen?" Bunz said, looking back at her dogs going bananas from the love Jen was giving them. "This is my home girl Andrea."

"Hey, girl, nice to meet you," Jen replied, with a head nod and a smile.

"'Drea, this is Jen; she's a sergeant at the prison up the street; the one dreads and fat-boy loudmouth died at."

Andrea gasped when she realized what Bunz was telling her.

"Sergeant Jen has agreed to spend her little lunch break with us," Bunz added.

"Oh… okay," Andrea replied, feeling somewhat confused.

Jen laughed as she sensed Andrea's apprehension.

"Bunz, yo' ass is crazy. I only needed that lame with the dreads taken out; why you hit that fat dude?"

Bunz shrugged. "I think I did whoever his cellmate was a favor. I bet my life that dude probably does nothin' but talk all day long with no off button."

"Oh, yeah. He was the most annoying person ever; he *stayed* tryna' holla at my staff 'n shit. Like, come on now, bro. He was fat as hell, had one eye, and a muthafuckin afro that was more a bird's nest due to that bald spot in back! And his fat-ass stank like a muhfucka, for cryin' out loud!"

Bunz and Andrea laughed their asses off.

"I'm for real," Sergeant Jen said, as she stroked behind Deuce's ears. "Fam, I searched his cell before; there was shit stains on the fucking toilet seat, dirt and hair on the floor, unwashed bowls with bugs in them on the table, and some green shit growin' out of the walls, and it was *not* mold!" Jen shuddered at the memory. "That's why I became a unit sergeant, so I can send peon officers to go search booty cells."

The girls laughed even harder.

"So, is the prison on lock-down?" Bunz asked, as her laughter began to die down.

"For now. Standard protocol, but neither of them muthafuckas were important; they were just numbers, and everyone knew King's time was limited. They dun' got scraped up off the track, and a worker crew came and power-washed it off. People are talkin' about it, but for the most part, don't nobody really give a fuck. Muthafuckas there just tryna get high."

"Hmmmm. Well, I have your goodie bag here, madam sergeant," Bunz told her.

After getting a head nod, Andrea handed the bag back to Jen. She unzipped it and saw ten kilos of cocaine, five kilos of heroin, and five bricks of fentanyl, along with five zip-loc bags filled with ecstasy and molly.

"This shit right here… *ooooooweeee!* Yo, this shit here, girl, this shit is worth *ten times* in prison as it's worth on the streets! It's like American money in Mexico! *Check!*"

Bunz chuckled at Jen again. "See you in a week, Sarge. Hit my line if you need anything else."

"You already know, boo-boo. Bye, 'Drea. It was nice meeting you."

"You, too, Jen," Andrea replied.

Jen kissed Deuce and LaLa on their noses then she got out with the bag, hopping back into her Benz. She pulled off with a quarter million dollars' worth of drugs that she and her crew of corrections staff planned to flood their prison with to all those who just couldn't cope with doing hard time, or soft time.

"We have one more stop to make before we go home," Bunz said, pulling off. "and be aware, 'Drea... this is *not* normal, what you are about to see."

Andrea furrowed her brows, puzzled as to what Bunz meant. Instead of asking, she decided to just wait and see for herself.

***

Austin paced back and forth in his living room. The arm pits of the pin-striped dress shirt he had on were drenched with sweat. He scratched the top of his balding head. He was beyond finicky about the hair-raising predicament he was in.

Half an hour past the time he had been expecting his visitor to come, he heard the doorbell chime. Hurrying to the front door, he undid all six of the locks and opened it. There at the door, he saw a very beautiful woman there. Her skin was the color of caramel, and she had golden dreadlocks, balled up and sitting on the top of her head. She had on a sexy skin-tight leather outfit, with stiletto pumps on her feet. In her hand, she was holding a book bag.

With her, Austin saw a young-looking white girl that had jet-black hair up in a high ponytail. She was garbed in a sexy green leather dress, fitted with gold studs. Austin could tell she was wearing stockings with the sexy gold heels on her feet.

"Wow," he said, stunned by how beautiful the women were, "Are you... uh...?"

"We're auditors, Mr. Levine. Care to invite us in?" the woman with the dreads asked him.

"Sure... um... yeah... come in."

He stepped to the side and the ladies entered, stepping into the living room. He shut the door behind them, locked it, and joined them.

"So, Austin." The dread head started speaking to him, setting the book bag on his long couch, "The job you have requested to be handled, it is... very different from the normal thing that I do."

"I just want my laptop back! Please! It has a *lot* of very sensitive data on it!"

"Like, gay porn?" the girl in the leather dress said, with a sly smile. "That *you* star in, with young, underaged boys?" she added.

Austin gasped. "N-No! It's not me! I'm a twin! I-I... it's experimental! I'm researching the world of homosexuality!"

The woman in the dress laughed. "By having sex with little boys?"

"And by putting a hit out on one of your *young partners*, that is demanding you pay him $50,000 dollars or he'll go to the media and the cops?" the dread head chick added.

Austin dropped his head in shame. "Please help me...I'll pay you more than your normal price if this stays between us."

"Okay," said dreads. "I'll need $100,000, all up front, right now."

Austin gasped. "$100,000?"

"Yep. I did my research, player. You got it. Go on and fetch before I get upset," she told him.

He looked at the girl in the dress.

"Scoot," she told him.

61

Austin rushed off to his bedroom, where he had a large old school safe. He hurried to get it opened then pulled out all the cash he had inside. He put together ten paper-banded stacks, each of them $10,000. He put the rest of the money back in and shut the safe door. Running back out to where the women were waiting, he handed the cash to the girl in the dress.

"It's all there! 100 grand! Can we get started now?"

"Anabelle? Can you please make sure that it equals 100 grand, and that all the bills are real?"

He saw the girl in the dress's eyes go wide. She didn't argue. She got to it, taking the cash to a table and ripping the bands. She counted each bill, making sure they were real in the process. Ten minutes later, she gave the dread head chick a thumbs up.

"Great! Now let's get to work," Austin pleaded again.

"Indeed, we shall my man," dreads said, before she went to her handbag.

Austin watched her pull out a semi-automatic Sig Sauer with a silencer screwed in the barrel. Then she looked at him. Austin's heart dropped when she cocked it, then pointed it at him.

"Hey! Wh-What are you doing?" he asked in fear, backing away from her.

Without even so much as a thought about it, dreads fired a round, hitting him in his stomach. He yelped in pain, falling backwards to the floor. He grasped at the wound as blood poured out, staining his shirt.

"What the hell lady?" he shouted, feeling more pain than he had ever felt in his life.

Dreads stepped and stood right over him. She put a finger to her lips and shushed him.

"Your gay partner contacted me *first* and he paid me *more* to kill *your* dumbass, *sooooo*…" She pointed the gun at his face and smirked, "highest bid *always* wins."

"*N-*"

PFFT! PFFT! PFFT! PFFT! PFFT!

Five to the face blew the top of his head off. His brains flew out, splattering all over the carpeted surface. Bunz looked down at his pushed-in face then looked up at Andrea. She nodded her head in the direction of the door.

Andrea went and opened it. "Come on in, Johnny," she called out.

Johnny, a young white boy wearing an Abercrombie & Fitch t-shirt, tight skinny jeans, and open-toe sandals walked in with his long hair in a ponytail. Andrea closed the door behind him and watched him walk towards where Bunz stood over the dead body. He looked down at the man who had broadcasted him to the world in a way he hadn't been ready to be seen.

Andrea stayed quiet, watching Bunz. When she turned her head and nodded, Andrea started walking towards him.

Johnny turned around just as Andrea raised a silenced pistol of her own at his face. He jumped back, with wide terrified eyes.

"Wait! Hold up! I paid you to kill *him*! I paid *more*, like you said to do," he panicked.

"True," Bunz spoke up from where she was, "but I took his money, so you gotta go, too, buddy boy. *Buh-bye* now."

Andrea squeezed the trigger repeatedly, knocking his brains out and painting the wall behind him crimson. His body fell on top of his lover. Their blood mixed as they joined each other again in death.

"Good job. Now, we clean up," Bunz told Andrea, who was *ecstatic* to have just gotten her own first kill.

Quickly, Bunz grabbed a little cardboard box from her book bag and set it on top of Johnny's chest. She pushed the little button that was on the front of it, starting the timer.

"Last one out is a crispy bitch!" Bunz joked, then took off in her pricey pumps, running out of the house.

Andrea high-tailed it behind her, both reaching the sidewalk just as the homemade incendiary device exploded.

The blaze it caused instantly grew into a raging inferno. The windows blew out as fire whooshed out of them. By the time Bunz and Andrea reached the Bentayga, where Deuce and LaLa awaited them, the entire house was a ball of flames, destroying any evidence of them ever being there.

Chapter 9

On the way back to her house, Bunz stopped at a gas station in Zion, right on the corner of Lewis Avenue and 21st Street. She pulled in and parked at one of the open pumps. A few other people were getting gas. A mob of young guys were posted to the side of the store, smoking weed, talking shit to each other, laughing loudly.

Bunz killed the engine and got out with her debit card to top her tank off. Andrea sat back and listened to the music as Doja Cat's *Can't Wait* played.

"Ayye, lil mama! What's up?"

Andrea heard one of the young guys calling out. She looked and saw three of them were heading towards Bunz, looking like they were seeing a bad bitch that was likely DTF. Deuce and LaLa started growling and Andrea told them to relax. They quieted down but kept their eyes on the young dudes as they approached Bunz. Andrea grabbed Bunz's Sig Sauer P226 XFive and cocked it, ready to use it if she had to.

Bunz saw the youngsters approaching her. The dark-skinned one with his dreads in neat barrels, rocking designer clothes had a smile on his face that told her he thought he was that nigga that could not be turned down by any chick. His guys that were behind him, all had sneaky looks on their faces that gave Bunz the creeps.

"What up, though, shortie? I see you pullin' up in Bentley truck 'n shit, lookin' all sexy in the leather. You look like you supposed to be fuckin' wit' a nigga like me," he said, pulling out two wads of cash from the pockets of his pants that were *waaaaay* too tight for Bunz's liking.

Bunz chuckled at his attempt to woo her.

"I see that. Good job, young man, but I'm not interested," she told him, trying to be polite.

"Not interested? Shortie, I'm out here getting' money, and I'm fresh as hell."

"I hear you; not interested," Bunz repeated, "I'm a little busy, though, if you don't mind."

He gave her an incredulous look. "Too busy? Yo' ass ain't doin' shit but pumpin' gas! Check it out shortie," he said, not even registering the look of building frustration on her face from him calling her *shortie*, "if you had a nigga like me, you'd be flyin' around on Lear jets 'n shit. I'm *really* that nigga out here."

Bunz laughed at him.

He got pissed at her laughing. His guys even laughed, seeing that he was a joke in her eyes.

"Man, what the fuck is so funny, shortie?" the dread-head asked, with anger in his voice.

"You. Tryna' pull out a few dollars to woo a boss like *me*, when I'm pushin' a $380,000 SUV, on rims that cost another $30,000. Come on, now, lil' dude; it's a nice try, but we on two different levels. Tell yo' groupie niggas to help you pick yo' face up off the ground 'cause I'm not doin' it for you, *shortie*."

One of the guys behind the dread-head furrowed. "Hold up! Bitch, who the fuck you callin' a groupie?!" he demanded, taking a step towards her.

"Yeah, bitch?! You think 'cause you pushin' a Bentley truck that you the shit?!"

Bunz laughed, "Yes, I do."

Just then, the SUV started shaking. The sounds of barking inside made the youngsters look at the whip. They heard a door open, then close. They expected vicious Pit Bulls to come out but instead, they saw a sexy-ass white chick in a tight leather dress with a gun in her hand.

The people that were at other pumps, and the few that were coming out of the store, saw the confrontation unfolding. Nobody moved; they all stayed, wanting to see it go down so they could put it all on social media.

"You; *Mr. Too Tall*," Bunz said to the tall young dude that had brazenly called her out of her name, "please step forward. I'd like a word with you."

The other two, including the dread-head, watched the tall one walk towards her. The SUV still shook; the dogs inside barked and growled even angrier, obviously watching the man approach their human through the window.

He kept a mean-mug on his face as he approached her. He stopped about a foot away. Towering over her, he looked down into her eyes, trying to intimidate her.

"Fuck you want, shortie?!" he barked.

WHAM!

Faster than he even anticipated, Bunz shot a fist up and hit him right in his throat. He fell backwards and hit the gas-soaked ground, grasping at his Adam's apple, choking his ass off. The other two gasped while the people that were watching all started laughing, teasing, talking big shit while they recorded everything on their Smart phones.

Andrea laughed her ass off as Bunz went to help the young dude up off the ground. Reluctantly, he allowed her to help him up.

"You need to start respecting women; you came out of one, so disrespecting *me*, is like doing that to yo' momma," she schooled. "And secondly," she continued, splitting a look from him to his guys, "y'all lil' niggas need to stop wearing' them tight-ass pants. Ya'll gon' catch yeast infections if y'all don't. Tight pants are for women to accentuate their curves. Them muthafuckas don't allow y'all to take deep breaths."

Bunz left him where he stood looking stupid. Laughs still filled the air at the gas station and phones still recorded. The three young ones marched off, having gotten treated by a chick in pumps.

After Bunz hung the pump back up and capped her gas tank, she and Andrea hopped back up into the Bentayga. Bunz pulled off, leaving everyone at the BP astounded by how she just made the three young dumb motherfuckers tuck their tails.

***

Bunz picked her babies up from Tracy and dropped the duffel bag she had stashed in the wheel well of her SUV. Back at the house, Andrea got showered while Bunz found her a pop-out ensemble to go out with Tim and make every woman in the club hate on her.

After Andrea got out of the shower, Bunz put her in her makeup chair that was built into the walk-in closets custom makeup station. In just about an hour, Andrea had gone from beautiful plain girl to *Go Viral Magazine* vixen.

Andrea then slipped into the intricately designed white YSL shirt with black YSLs monogrammed all over it, a low cleavage line with a backless rear, and strings woven in through the sides. With it, Bunz chose a shiny black leather micro-mini YSL skirt that she knew would hug Andrea's blessed hips and ass perfectly.

From Bunz's sense in fashion and her personal experience, she had relayed to Andrea that most men *loved* women in sexy pantyhose, so Andrea got out a fair of black fishnets that had roses woven in to go with the sexy outfit, then she paired it all with white leather YSL knee-high stiletto boots that were studded with jewels.

Bunz spritzed some YSL perfume on Andrea then pulled her in front of the full-body mirror. Andrea gasped when she saw how Bunz had made her look worthy of the BET Awards.

"Timmy is gonna' end up wifin' you, 'Drea," Bunz told her, amazed by how gorgeous she was.

"I may be young, but I don't think I'm too young to become the wife of a good man, Bunz." Andrea looked at her then, "Thank you; you have no idea how much this means to me."

Bunz nodded her head. "It helps that you have heart and know how to use a gun already," she chuckled. "Nonetheless, I am gonna' turn you into the *baddest* bitch to ever walk the earth."

"I think that ship has sailed due to you, Bunz," Andrea said then.

"Aww!" Bunz gushed at the compliment. "Come here, you!"

She pulled Andrea into her arms and hugged her like a loving big sister.

"I want to help you get that bitch back for what she did to Eric, Bunz. I don't care what I have to do. I am *down*."

Bunz drew back and looked at how serious Andrea looked. She nodded her head, appreciating the willingness to help.

"Thank you, 'Drea, but that one is my battle. I need to be the one to see her bleed. That whore is gonna' feel pain that makes childbirth feel like it fucking *tickles*."

***

At 10:00 on the dot, Tim was spotted on Bunz's high-tech motion camera system, pulling into the driveway in his red Mansory edition Ferrari 812 Superfast. Bunz got up to let Tim in. Tim stepped into the foyer fresh as hell, in a monogrammed Fendi fit with the sneakers to match. In his ears were yellow-diamond studs and around his neck were two yellow-gold Cuban link chains, each of them with a diamond charm, and on his wrist was a yellow-gold Rolex with diamonds all over it.

Bunz gave him a hug and welcomed him into her home. He saw LaLa and Deuce laid out on the floor around a bear fur rug. Laying on the fluffy rug was Eric Jr. and Monique, both kicking and giggling at each other.

"Ayyee, look at my niece and my nephew!" he exclaimed, always happy to see the babies. He hurried over to where they were and kneeled next to them to play with them. "Sis, they're like the most perfect mix of you and E," he told Bunz, making goofy faces at the two, making them giggle even louder, "I can see bro and you in the both of them."

Bunz smiled. "Strong genes, I guess. So, you takin' her to your spot, or somewhere else?"

"My spot. I figure I could make a better impression on her if we go somewhere that provides the best service; where better than my own club?"

"True. Don't get to thinkin' she needs to have money flashed in her face, though. One thing I've seen in her, is that she ain't no gold diggin' bitch, you feel me?"

He nodded his head. "I swear on E's grave, Bunz, I won't do her wrong. I'm yo' top employee, so anything and everything I do represents your choice in puttin' me where I am. You already know how I get down in the streets, but I'm ready to be a man instead of a player... if things go good between her and I."

Just before Bunz could reply, they both heard the tapping of high heels. Looking to where the steps that led to the upstairs were, Bunz and Tim saw her. Tim's eyes went as wide as dinner plates when he saw Andrea. He was awestruck by the chick. He had seen so many gorgeous women, fucked many of them, and had so many of them pining for him, but Andrea was the type that he had always wanted; the scared vulnerable chick that could be turned into a real soldier, while remaining humble.

"Now *that* is the type of woman that *I* want in *my* life, Bunz," Tim said as he feasted his eyes on the Italian beauty garbed in the sexiest cranberry-colored ensemble.

"Play yo' cards right, and she will be," Bunz told him.

Tim went to her, meeting her at the bottom step. Andrea smiled down at him as he took her hand.

"Hey, gorgeous." Tim gave her a hug and a kiss on her cheek. "You're lookin' like you ready to turn *the* fuck up tonight."

"Oh, I most definitely am, handsome," Andrea replied, with a big flirty smile on her face. "Bye, Bunz, Eric Jr., Monique, LaLa, and Deuce!"

Andrea nearly dragged Tim out of the house, leaving Bunz inside laughing her ass off.

Chapter 10

Tim turned his 'Rarri into the nearly filled parking lot of the club. Andrea saw the name '*Club Racine*' above the entrance. She took it all in already able to see how lit it was. The line damn near wrapped around the building while people waited, impatiently, to get inside.

All eyes were on the expensive special edition Ferrari as Tim pulled up to the front door. Andrea wondered why he was doing that, instead of finding a parking spot. The question left her mind when she saw a group of girls breaking their necks to get a good look at the car, likely dying to see what baller was going to hop out, and which one of them would he choose to accompany him inside. Andrea couldn't *wait* to hop out and piss them all off.

Tim opened his door and got out. The head bouncer made his way over as Tim opened the door for Andrea to get out.

"Tim! Hey Tim!" a random woman in the front called out until she saw him grab Andrea's hand and assist her out of the car.

Andrea couldn't help but smile her ass off as the woman went from trying to get his attention, to cursing angrily, pissed that the rich Black man had a white girl with him.

Tim dapped the bouncer up, then extended his elbow out for Andrea. She looked her arm through it and allowed him to escort her inside.

***

Kendrick Lamar's *Not Like Us* blared from the speakers inside and people shouted the words turning up with drinks in hand.

"*Holy shit Tim! It's really poppin' in this bitch!*" Andrea hollered close to his ear over the music and the people rapping with the famed Compton rapper.

"I see," Tim said back, in her ear. "I'm happy every time I come up in here; this was a very good investment I made."

Andrea gasped. "This is *your* club?"

He nodded. "Yeah. I went half on it with one of my homegirls," he told her.

An instant flash of jealousy hit Andrea. She already didn't like the idea of any other chick being involved in Tim's inner circle, except for Bunz.

"But," he began to add. "I bought her half when she started doin' the drugs we sold. Couldn't have her cluckin' out all over the place and makin' us *both* look bad."

"Where is she now?" Andrea asked.

"Dead. She trusted the wrong guy one night when she came to handle some 'biz; she met dude here and ended up doin' some coke with him. His shit had fentanyl in it. I'm sure you know the rest."

Andrea shook her head, sad to hear it. Everybody was dying from fentanyl overdoses.

"Did the guy get arrested and charged for her death?" she asked, as Tim led her over towards the bar for drinks.

"Nope. He dead, too."

"Overdose?" Andrea thought.

Tim looked at her. "Nope."

He gave no further explanation. She didn't need one.

At the bar, two beautiful Puerto Rican women were keeping the drinks flowing to all the clubbers. They got super excited when they saw Tim approaching. They nearly got into it, trying to be the one that served him.

"Ladies, relax," he told them, as Andrea considered diving over the bar and giving them both a Bacardi-bottle stamp on their faces. "My lovely lady friend here and I will have plenty of requests for the night. No need to tear each other up."

The ladies looked at Andrea. Both curled their lips up at the white girl.

"¿Por qué muchas gueras siempre intentan estar con hombres morenos y latinos? the one with her long dark hair in stylish cornrows asked the other, glaring at Andrea.

While the other one, whom had dark red hair mean-mugged Andrea, she said, "No lo sé, pero cuando la puta vaya al baño, la estoy siguiendo y la voy a joder."

Andrea busted out laughing at them, causing Tim to furrow his eyebrows in confusion. She knew that the girls were questioning why a white girl seemingly always wanted a dark-skinned Latino man. And the second girl had threatened to do physical harm to her.

"Escuchame bien*, putas.*" *Listen to me carefully, bitches*, Andrea said, throwing back their Spanish-speaking sneak dissing. "Puede que sea una chica blanca, pero hablo un poco de español. Asi que, cuando voy al baño y quieras entrar y tratarme, meteré tu cabeza en el maldito indoor y tiraré de la cadena, perra. ¡Tratame!," *I may be a white girl, but I speak a little Spanish. So, when I go to the bathroom and you wanna come in and treat me, I'm gonna stick your head in the fucking toilet and flush the toilet, bitch. Treat me!* she then dared the two.

Taken aback by Andrea, the Boricuas both took steps back, shocked speechless by how Andrea had just fucked their heads up and issued a threat of her own in Spanish. Tim busted out laughing at the salty looks on the girls' faces.

"I don't speak nothin' but money, but it sounds like you just treated they asses," he said to Andrea.

"I kindly told those two lovely ladies that they shouldn't underestimate a white girl. Now, how about that drink, handsome," Andrea said, with a seductive smile on her face.

***

"*Ooooohhh, Ruuubiiooooo*! Shit! Oh, God!," Paula cried out, as her Italian stallion fucked her hard and fast from the back in the parking lot of a big movie theatre out in Racine.

She had her hands on the engine hood of his limited-edition Lamborghini Aventador SVJ. The heat from the big V12 engine that laid under the clear top had her hands hot and sweaty, but not as hot and sweaty as Rubio had her.

The silver silk button-down Hermes shirt she had on was open, allowing her red lace bra with her perky little breasts to show. Her tiny leather Hermes skirt was up around her waist, her thong was to the side, and inside of her was 7-inches of hard Italian dick, beating her guts up.

She had been unable to resist Rubio in his custom-cut Armani suit, with his custom Cartier watch on his wrist. Everything about him screamed sophisticated GQ gangster. Just looking at him kept her pussy dripping wet.

After a delicious seven-course meal at her new Mediterranean cuisine restaurant in downtown Racine, Rubio had taken her to a movie up close to the highway. When they left out, Paula couldn't help herself. She was feeling frisky and she was not a patient enough a woman to wait until they got to his mansion.

She wanted the dick and she wanted it right there and then. Rubio was all too happy to oblige her request. He lived for the chance to slut the little bitch out wherever and whenever she wanted.

"Ohh, yeah, baby," groaned Rubio as he gripped her hips and pounded her like he was a jackhammer breaking up an old concrete sidewalk. "I *love* the way you feel!"

"Rubio! I... oooooo, God! I'm gonna cum, baby! Oh shit!" Paula announced, feeling a strong one coming on.

Rubio went harder. He grabbed her hair and pulled her head back. He fucked her harder and faster, ignoring the group of young teenagers that were walking past, pointing at them, laughing and clowning around. Seconds later, Paula cried out at the tops of her lungs, then she came hard, all over Rubio's dick.

Rubio grunted and cursed. He felt his own nut coming. His back muscles started getting tighter and tighter by the second. His nuts tingled and Paula could feel his cock spasming inside of her. She wanted to finish him off the way she felt a good woman always got her man there.

"Voglio succhiarti il cazzo adesso," she told him in Italian.

Quickly, she reached back, pulled him out of her, then she spun to him, dropped down and opened her mouth wide, sticking her tongue out. Rubio grabbed her head, stuck his dick in her mouth, and started face-fucking her. His balls slapped her chin repeatedly. He cursed, squeezing his eyes closed.

A car rode up and stopped. The teenagers inside all filmed Paula on her knees with a dick in her mouth. The animalistic sounds that Rubio made as his nut came closer to busting made them all laugh. The two ignored the youngsters; it was all about them and the hot public acts that made them go crazy over each other.

"*Fuuuck!*" Rubio roared right as he came.

Paula gripped his dick with one hand and started jerking him as his nut exploded in her mouth. She milked him for every last drop, then put on a show for him by spitting it all back out on his dick and slurping it back up.

"Wooo! Yeah, you nasty little bitch! Lick all of it back up, whore," he demanded of her.

Paula loved it when he talked like that to her. It aroused her to no end. She obeyed and swallowed when it was all back in her mouth.

"Mmmmm. Tasty!" she purred, looking up at him, with liquid desire in her eyes.

Rubio looked over at the car, that was still there.

"Oh shit! Dude, go!" yelled one of the boys inside.

The driver hit the gas and peeled off, bending the corner quick and disappearing.

Rubio took his chick by the hand and pulled her up from the ground. He fixed her thong, pulled her skirt back down, then after he buttoned her shirt back, he tongued kissed her, not caring at all that his sperm had just been in her mouth. Paula moaned as his kiss set her on fire again. When he let off, she was on fire.

"I have a lot of energy still," he told her. "Let's go find something to do."

Her eyes lit up as an idea came to her mind. "Hey! There's this club right down the road! We can go there, have a few drinks, fuck in the bathroom, then go home and fuck each other to sleep!"

Rubio grinned. "I like that idea. Let's go."

He got her into the passenger's seat of his Lambo, hopped in behind the wheel. He started the engine and peeled off, burning rubber out of the parking lot, making every eye that had come out of the movie theatre wish they could afford such a car like his.

***

Bunz laid on her side on her big canopy bed. Her babies were both sleeping soundly next to her. Nearly 300 pounds of dog were laid out on the other side of them. Ashanti's harmonious voice crooned through the wireless surround-sound system in her massive bedroom.

On the giant 88-inch 4K HDTV that was mounted on the wall across from the bed, the old love movie *Love and Basketball* was on. She sighed to herself. Watching the ending made her think of Eric. Neither one of them were athletes, but the undying love that was between the two in the movie made her think of what she and Eric had. It had been so strong that even after she had left him high and dry, when she showed back up at his home, in a stolen pick-up truck that she killed a man for, Eric had accepted her right back into his life and made her problems his.

There was no other man that was for her. With him gone, she buried her heart. Content on staying single for the rest of her life, all she cared about was raising the two little ones that came into the world from the realest love ever.

***

The doorbell rang as the movie ended. The dogs immediately rose up, ears perked up alert and ready to protect. Bunz grabbed her iPhone and brought up the camera in the doorbell. When she saw who was there, she went rigid.

What the fuck?! This bitch must *have a death wish*, she thought to herself, and got up as gently as she could, so as to not wake her kids.

"LaLa come; Deuce, stay!" she told them.

The female Bullie trailed behind her while the Alpha male stayed with the babies. Bunz ran into her walk-in closeted and hurried to grab the fully automatic Heckler & Koch G36, fitted with a silencer and a 100-round drum.

She ran barefoot to the door, ready to make the bitch that had the balls to show up at her home, after Bunz had held her responsible for what happened to Eric, bleed to death on the front porch.

Chapter 11

The woman at the door was fair skinned with long luscious raven hair. She stood 5'2" in the flats she had on her feet. She was dressed in tight-fitting plaid pajama bottoms, a t-shirt with a teddy bear on it, and a fluffy robe. She looked as if she had just rolled out of bed and hopped into the new Rolls-Royce Wraith that she had just pulled up in. Her eyes were puffy and blood-shot red, with dark rings around them.

She looked horrible, haggard. Bunz could care less. The second she opened the door, she put the barrel of her spitter in the Persian diamond connoisseur's face. The girl immediately gasped, jumping back in fear.

LaLa growled viciously, standing at Bunz's side, anxious to be put to work. She stood poised and ready to pounce like a hungry lioness with a whole pride of hungry relatives to feed.

"You got three seconds to say why the fuck you are here, then you die," Bunz told the girl, aiming right at her remarkably beautiful face.

"Bunz." Sonia started sobbing, voice breaking up as tears fell from her eyes. "He... he... he was like my brother! It wasn't s-supposed to end this way!"

"*But it did, bitch!*" Bunz stepped out and put the silencer so close to Sonia's nose that she could smell the gun powder. "*You called that bitch and set us up!*"

"Eric *told* me to! I swear to God! He felt like it would draw her out from wherever she was hiding, Bunz! I'm sorry! I am so sorry!"

Sonia then broke down, crying her eyes out. She fell to her knees at Bunz's feet, begging her to forgive her. She let it all out, unable to hold any of it in any longer.

Sonia had grown up with Bunz's would-have-been husband. She loved Eric like they were a part of the same gene pool. The flawless diamonds that Bunz had robbed and killed Barry the Diamond Man for, Sonia had purchased them for a whopping $165 million, after Eric had reached out to her to help Bunz get the hot rocks off.

It was known that killing the well-connected mobster had gotten prices put on Bunz's head. When Bunz met Sonia for the first time, at a well-known southern restaurant down in Chicago, the Persian beauty had no problem doing business with her, on the strength of her and Eric's long-time kinship. But, unbeknownst to Bunz, Eric had Sonia use her connections to get in contact with Paula Paulmatti's people, to facilitate a fake return of the diamonds, for more than what she paid Bunz, and, said she would supply the mobster's daughter with Bunz's whereabouts.

In no way shape or form did Sonia want to do it, little did Bunz know, but because Eric wanted her to, Sonia did it. And it backfired, like a broke-ass Harley Davidson in need of some serious engine work.

Bunz sighed. Tears had run down her face. Her heart broke for Sonia, because deep in her heart, knowing that Eric had a *very* keen sense of good and bad, when it came to people, she had to admit to herself that there was *no way* that Sonia would hurt Eric, nor someone that she knew he loved dearly. She lowered her gun. Sensing her anger subsiding, LaLa started settling down as well. Bunz reached down and took Sonia's hand, pulling her up off the ground.

"Come in," Bunz told her. "I'll get you a drink and we can talk."

Sonia wiped her tears away, then nodded her head. She followed Bunz into the house, with XXL Bully eyes on her. Bunz closed the door, locked it then led Sonia into her kitchen.

***

Andrea twerked her ass all in Tim's crotch. She was going crazy as Migo's *Bad and Boujee* with Lil' Uzi. Towards the back of the dance floor, they were surrounded by so many others getting wild on the floor.

For three more songs, the two danced, vibing with each other. They were in tune with each other, feeling like their hearts were beating at the same time.

Andrea needed a break and a drink. She took Tim's hand and led him through the crow towards the bar. Right before she got there, another chick bumped into her, spilling the drink she had in her hand all over her silk shirt.

"What the fuck you clumsy cunt?" the girl yelled as the pinkish stain began to spread, "This shirt cost more than your whole fucking wardrobe!"

Andrea was seconds away from chin-checking the girl, when recognition set in. She saw the lady's face and gasped in shock. Tim stepped up to intervene when he saw Andrea's face. A man stepped up at the young chick's side, with a mean-mug on his face.

"Looks like someone owes my girl a new shirt," the guy said, looking at Tim with hard narrowed eyes.

Time craned his neck, with an incredulous look on his face. Andrea was still stuck, staring at the woman. She could not believe who she was looking at.

"How about we recognize this as an accident, and let it go?" Tim suggested.

"Or," the guy countered, closing the gap between him and Tim, standing nearly half a foot taller than him, "you can cough up some loot so my girl can get a new shirt! *Now!*"

"Hmmmm. I *really* like *my* idea better, my dude," Tim replied, smiling at the guy.

Andrea was finally able to take her eyes off the chick and look at Tim, though the girl was still glaring at her.

"Rubio! Kick this motherfucker's ass for bein' with such a fucking klutz," she demanded.

"Tim. It's okay," Andrea went to pull him away from the big Italian. "Let it go. It's not worth the moment."

Tim nodded and took a step back.

"Yeah, guy! Listen to your little whore! You're more of a bitch than *she* is! Men, *real* men, tell women what to do, *not* the other way around!"

People that were around them had heard the heated words and were all in the mix. Some backed up, expecting fists to start flying, and maybe even a gun to come out and get to barking. Others stayed right where they were, dying to see it go down.

"I hear you talkin', bruh," said Tim, eying the guy as Andrea pulled him away. "See you a little later, though. Enjoy your night while you can."

"Keep walking asshole, if I see you or your whore again I'm going to kick your ass," the man yelled into the air.

Paula grinded her teeth in anger as she watched the dude and his clumsy bitch walk off. She looked down at her ruined Christian Dior shirt. She stomped her Dior stiletto pump furiously on the floor.

"Don't worry, babe," Rubio told her, giving her ass a smack. "If I see that son of a bitch in the parking lot, I'll kick his ass for you, then I'll take whatever he's got in his pockets."

"I wanna beat the *piss* out of the bitch for bumping into me! Who the fuck does she think that she is?!" Paula snapped.

"Let's go get us a drink and get back into party mode. We'll see them before the night is over."

***

Bunz took a sip of her tea as she watched Sonia's eyes water up again. The twins sucked on their pacifiers, feet kicking wildly, as Sonia hovered over them. It was her first time seeing the babies of her big bro. After Bunz had been abducted, Sonia heard, that somehow, Bunz had escaped then she went into hiding and hadn't been heard from until a few months prior. Sonia tracked her down after hearing about the shooting at the restaurant. She had a hunch that if such a catastrophic ordeal had happened, involving the Paulmatti family, it had to be Bunz. She didn't know yet, but soon would, that Sonia had gone to Tracy's house and got Bunz' location.

Sonia was elated yet devastated to not be sharing the moment with her brother. Seeing the precious baby boy and girl had her emotions so jumbled up.

"Eric Jr., Monique; I'm your Auntie Sonia," she wept, kissing two of her fingers and touching their foreheads, "It is so nice to finally meet you. I love you two so much, and so does your mommy, and your daddy does, too."

Bunz smiled. The words that Sonia spoke tugged at her heart. She wished Eric was there. She wished that they could be there as a family.

The sound of her phone dinging brought Bunz out of her daze. She went and grabbed it from her dresser. She saw it was a text from Andrea.

Reading it, Bunz immediately saw red. Her blood started boiling. She grew hot with rage.

"Sonia."

The Persian belle looked over at Bunz. "Yeah? Everything okay?" she asked, seeing a murderous look on Bunz's face.

"No. We're goin' for a ride… *right now!*"

***

83

Tee Grizzley's *IDGAF* featuring Chris Brown and Mariah The Scientist blared. The couples in the club danced closely together, packing the dance floor. Andrea and Tim danced with each other while keeping their eyes open. Tim wanted to handle the Italian right now, but he'd been taught by Bunz to have patience. Driving too fast always caused accidents.

The two that they had words with were at the bar, sipping, touching, and flirting with each other. Every so often, they would glance over at Andrea and Tim, then they would look away. After three more songs, Andrea got the text that she had been waiting for. She showed it to Tim. He started grinning, geeked up.

"You ready?" she asked him.

"I *been* ready," he told her, still eying the big slick-talker.

He then pulled Andrea and he pressed his lips to hers. Andrea was shocked by the move, but in no way did she pull back. She moaned from the feeling of being in his arms with his lips on hers. It felt magical to her. When he started parting her lips with his tongue, and stuck it into her mouth, Andrea nearly creamed her panties.

Tim tongued her down right where they stood. The club was hot and he heated her up even more. She felt like she was melting, like her knees were going to give out at any second. Their lips boxed and their tongues danced with each other, as if Mariah and Tee Grizzley made the song just for them. Andrea could not remember ever having felt so safe and cared for in her entire life.

After a minute more, Andrea's thong was soaking wet. Her juices leaked and her pantyhose were dripping wet, and she could feel it in between her thighs. Her nipples were erect, aching, and pointing at whose mouth they wanted on them. Tim pulled back a few more seconds later. He smiled at her, still holding her in his arms. He stroked her soft cheek with his thumb, caressing her unbelievably beautiful face.

"Let's do this, gorgeous," Tim told her.

Andrea nodded her head, then let him take her hand, and he led her through the crowd, heading for the exit.

***

"They're leaving! Come on!," Rubio urged, eager to catch the guy out in the parking lot.

Paula slammed her last shot of Patron and hopped off her stool, ready to catch the bitch and beat her senseless.

Rubio led the way to the exit and stepped out with his woman right behind him.

They both looked around for the two. A loud whistle came. They looked to their right in the direction the whistle had come from, and saw the guy, and the chick, standing in front of a Ferrari.

"Show time, baby," said Rubio, cracking his knuckles.

He and Paula started towards the two, ready to throw hands.

"I cannot *wait* to see you kick his ass, baby," Paula said, with a smirk, following her man to what she knew was going to be a blood bath.

Chapter 12

Tim and Andrea waited patiently for the couple to get to them. To the left was a windowless van waiting just as they had planned. When Paula and Rubio made it about halfway to them the van pulled around cutting off their sight on the other couple.

BOCKA! BOCKA! BOCKA! BOCKA! BOCKA!

Rubio fired at the van's windshield repeatedly while backing Paula up behind him. The van didn't stop. It didn't even slow down.

"Fuck!" Rubio shouted when he ran out of bullets, "Go Paula, run!"

Paula took off running like she wasn't wearing high heels. She ran towards his Lambo with the key fob in her hand. Rubio was right behind her, wishing he had an extended clip.

They could hear the van's engine gunning as they weaved through a row of parked cars. Suddenly, a tall muscular figure wearing a ski-mask, hopped up from the side of a car, with a machete in his hand.

Paula screamed and slipped, falling to the ground.

"Paula!" Rubio hollered, trying to get to her.

He didn't see the deadly weapon in the guy's hand. The mysterious man saw Paula on the ground but heard Rubio coming. In the blink of an eye, when Rubio got close enough, the man swung the machete *hard*.

It took Rubio a millisecond to process seeing the blade come at him but by then it was too late. The blade sliced right through the center of Rubio's face, going through the middle of his nose to the back of his head, severing the whole top half of his head completely off.

The split wig and his brain flew in different directions, landing on two separate cars. Rubio's lifeless body dropped, hitting the ground and spewing out blood.

The masked man turned back to get Paula... but she was gone.

***

Both Bunz and Sonia gasped in shock when they saw the masked stranger appear from out of thin air and cut Rubio's head off. Bunz slammed on the brakes, stuck in disbelief.

"Who the hell is *that?*" Sonia asked in bewilderment, clutching the automatic Uzi that she had gotten from Bunz's cache of weapons.

"I... I don't know," Bunz replied, still stunned.

"HH-hey Bunz! Paula is getting away!" Sonia shouted.

Bunz looked at where Sonia was pointing. She saw the girl hop into a Lamborghini and peel off.

"*Fuck!*" Bunz shouted.

She mashed the gas to go catch her.

"Bunz, wait! The kids!" Sonia reminded her.

Strapped to their baby car seats in the mid-section of the van, Eric Jr. and Monique were tucked under there blankets, sound asleep still. LaLa and Deuce were lying next to them, looking up at Bunz, wondering what the heck was going on.

Bunz knew it was pointless to chase a Lambo in a Chevy van and too dangerous to do it with her babies in tow. She muttered a curse under her breath, seeing Paula dip out of the lot. She was heated, but just then, Tim's Ferrari sped past her, blazing towards the exit.

"Come on, come on, come *ooooon*, Tim!" Andrea urged as he shot up out of the parking lot, hopping onto Highway 20 to get on Paula's tail.

With his AK-47 pistol in her hands, loaded with a drum fitting one hundred rounds, Andrea refused to let Bunz's tears go unanswered for.

Tim had the Aventador's brake lights in his view. He used every bit of horsepower the souped-up V12 engine had to catch up. Andrea felt herself trembling with anticipation and giddiness as Tim broke speeds of more than 168 miles an hour.

Suddenly, a black crotch-rocket shot past them as if they weren't even moving. Flames shot out of the exhaust pipes. The rider was tucked low, wind sailing right over their helmet.

"Is that...?" Andrea went to ask Tim.

"I think so... but who the fuck *is* he?" Tim wondered, as the rider created a wide gap between them.

Right after he asked, the window to his Ferrari shattered, and two explosions in the front of the car came. The front end started skidding on bare rims from the tires being blown out. Tim caught a glimpse of muzzle flashes coming from the driver's side of the Aventador. Andrea screamed in panic.

Keeping his car under control, Tim was able to bring his Ferrari to a safe stop. He cursed angrily as Paula got away. The crotch-rocket, though, was still pursuing her, weaving in and out, dodging bullets like it was nothing.

***

BOC! BOC! BOC! BOC! BOC! BOC! BOC! BOC! BOC! BOC!

Paula emptied the clip to the semi-automatic Springfield Armory Hellcat, dumping all seventeen rounds out of her window at the motorcycle rider as she got closer to I-94. She wasn't sure if she'd hit the people in the Ferrari, but whatever she did stopped the car dead in its tracks. But the bike was still on her ass, and now she was out of bullets.

"Motherfucker!" she shouted, tossing the gun over to the passenger's seat.

The crotch-rocket was gaining on her. She could hear its engine now, screaming over the Lambo's engine.

Panicking, Paula frantically tried to figure out what she could do. Up ahead, she knew that the area alongside the highway had some stores, gas stations, hotels, and a couple of truck stops, but it was still a quarter mile away.

She kept her foot planted to the floor. The speedometer read 193 miles an hour. The crotch-rocket was still on her tail. Two minutes later, the business area came into view. She saw the truck stop up on her left at the traffic light. Parked at the perimeter of its parking lot, Paula saw a bunch of Racine County Sheriff vehicles parked in a row.

"Yes!" she shouted with relief.

She let off the gas to slow up but kept her eye on the bike. It shot over into the fast lane, attempting to run up on her driver's side. She swerved over and cut it off. It tried to go left. She stopped it again.

Coming in on the intersection, the bright lights of the businesses illuminating the whole strip, Paula caught sight of the rider pulling out a gun in the driver's side mirror.

Throwing all caution to the limit, Paula swerved hard to her left and shot through the center of the highway, entering the on-coming lanes. Beeping the horn, she did everything she could to start attracting anyone's attention that may be outside.

Paula reached the intersection and shot through it, nearly getting t-boned by a semi as it was attempting to make a wide left turn onto 20. She slammed on her brakes, trying to slow down, but started skidding and spinning. She spun right into the gas station's lot, narrowly missing slamming into one of the sheriff cars. She came to a stop and jumped out, screaming for her when she saw the cops inside of the store, drinking coffee.

BRRRRRRRRRRRRRRRRRRRRRRRRRRRRRRRRRRRRRR!

Shots came flying at the gas station. People that had been outside had dove and ducked for cover as what sounded like a machine gun got to firing. Windows exploded, cars and SUVs were hit up.

Paula hit the floor just as a barrage had flown right over here, entering the store and hitting a coffee machine.

Covering herself, Paula heard the crotch-rocket whiz by. The rider beeped the horn, then as the sheriff deputies ran out of the store with their guns drawn, they went to fire at the rider. But he was gone before any of them could get a shot off.

***

Bunz parked the van in the back of her big garage. Sonia sat quietly in the front seat, still bamboozled by it all. Tim and Andrea were in the back with the babies and the dogs, rendered speechless. Amongst them all, Bunz could not even begin trying to process any of it. She wasn't even sure if any of it really happened but seeing that she was in Eric's '*work*' van, something had to have happened.

I freakin' had the bitch… I had her… how in the actual fuck did I fail? she asked herself, damn near ready to cry.

Inside, Bunz settled her disturbed twins down while Tim called his Ferrari in stolen. Andrea looked at the news media sites on her phone and saw more of what happened after she and Tim could no longer continue.

Sonia was on the phone with her people, trying to get someone tracking Paula from where she was seeing Paula at on the news, surrounded by Racine County Sheriff deputies at the Phillips 66 fueling station.

LaLa and Deuce sat at the side of Bunz's bed. LaLa, sensing Bunz's anguish and frustration. Deuce remained quiet but, the hair on his back stood up, displaying his own anger. He was enraged because his *human* was enraged. He wanted to kill because *she* wanted to kill. His alpha male instincts had kicked in. He could rip an angry bull apart by himself at that moment.

"I got people keeping an eye on where she goes from being with the pigs," Sonia told Bunz, entering the bedroom, "until the bitch is found and in pieces in some wild animal's stomach, I am not leaving your side."

Bunz nodded her head.

Tim came to the doorway, lightly tapping on it to get the ladies' attention. They both looked his way. He could see fire and smoke in the room.

"I'ma head home, y'all," he told them, so very heated about his $730,000 dollar Ferrari.

"Tim, you are *not* leaving. Get a room here. I don't know if the bitch knows that *I'm* responsible for all this and we *don't* know who the guy on the bike was, if he's just after her, or after her *then* at us," said Bunz. "I got every one of my hitters ready to go where I say when any of Sonia's people give us a location. Until then, we stay *together*; besides, I am *very* sure that 'Drea would appreciate your company for the night after all that shit."

Tim nodded his head. He understood exactly what Bunz was saying. He told them both good night, then went to find Andrea.

Sonia sat on the edge of the bed and sighed to herself. She rubbed her temples, trying to relieve the tension headache that had her head pounding.

"Get some sleep," Bunz told her, while she cradled Monique in her arms, while Eric Jr. laid next to her, awake but laying still and quiet. "We're gonna' have a *very* busy week ahead of us."

Nodding her head, Sonia got up. She gave the babies kisses on their foreheads, then hugged and kissed Bunz on her forehead. She patted the dogs, then went to find a room to lay down and close her eyes.

Bunz laid her tired daughter next to her brother, then she herself stretched out. She laid there, looking up at the ceiling for a while. Her eyes filled with tears. She was so angry with herself for fucking up something that was easier than many other things that she had done to put someone down. Her mind was racing, and her blood was still boiling. Not long after her babies fell asleep, Bunz passed out before she even realized that fatigue had set in.

Chapter 13

Andrea laid on her bed in her guest house above the garage. When she heard footsteps, she looked up and saw Tim coming. He looked horrible, like he hadn't slept in days and was pissed about it.

"You okay?" she asked him as he came and sat on the bed next to her.

Tim looked at her. "Not even close; we had that bitch in our hands. I fucked up so bad."

"Hey," Andrea sat all the way up and took his hand into hers, "do not blame yourself. That bitch is slippery and she went to the cops for help. *Any* smart person would have had to fall back when that happened. Trust and believe, there *will* be a next time, Tim."

Her words made him smile. He couldn't help but to respect and admire her optimism and he loved how she was ready to dump on the bitch herself.

"Beautiful, real, and a muthafuckin' gangsta, where have you been all my life?" Tim asked, enamored by Andrea.

Andrea smiled back. "Oh, a few homeless shelters, under bridges and tents, under other people's roofs only to get propositioned, then kicked out or jumped on when I refused dirty advances."

Tim frowned at that. He shook his head, unable to picture such a beautiful woman in such a fucked-up predicament. It was not what he had expected to hear.

"I'm sorry, 'Drea," he told her, meaning it whole heartedly.

He kicked his shoes off, then laid on the bed next to her, looking up at the dark star-lit sky through the glass ceiling. He sighed to himself, still tripped out by the events that had happened.

Andrea rolled over on top of him. She laid so that she was looking directly down into his eyes. Her arms were folded under her bosom, her eyes on his, her lips, curling up into a warm smile.

"You kissed me at the club," she said, thinking about it still.

Despite all the craziness, the kiss had been on her mind since their lips met. She could still damn near feel the tingling sensation that they had brought when they touched.

Tim smiled up at her. "You seem surprised by that."

She nodded her head. "It was… random."

"I was attempting to make them think that we were too drunk and horny to be aware of our surroundings."

"Oh." Andrea's smile began to fade. "Soo… it *wasn't* a real kiss then?"

He smiled again. "Did it *feel* like a real kiss?"

"Um… I don't think I remember; refresh my memory."

Andrea then found herself on her back, with Tim on top of her. She immediately grew aroused from the feeling of his hard heavy body on top of her. A second later, his lips found hers again. Andrea's eyes closed and she relished the feeling of true bliss that they brought to her.

He lifted after a few seconds and gazed into her eyes.

"Let me up," she then requested.

Tim rolled off her, hoping that he had not done something wrong. He sat up right and watched her get up off the bed. She went over to where the built-in home audio system was and turned it on.

Tim heard SZA's *Hit Different* featuring Ty Dolla $ign come on, crooning from the wireless speakers that were placed around the loft to provide studio-like sound.

Andrea went back over to where Tim laid. She clapped her hands. The lights dimmed to a deep red sensuous hue. She reached down to the hem of her shirt and pulled it off. She tossed it at Tim and reached back to unsnap her bra.

Tim's eyes went wide when he saw her mouth-watering melons, nipples erect and looking like they needed a mouth to suck on them. He watched her unbutton her little skirt, drop it to her ankles and step out of it. His dick grew hard as he drank in the sight of her beautiful body. Titties out, pantyhose on, the sight of her pearl-colored Cosa Bella thong through her rose-woven fishnets, and the sexy white stiletto boots had Tim ready to ravage her. The second she took her hair out of the high ponytail Tim could no longer just lay there. He hopped right up and rushed to her, dying to experience the love she had waiting for him.

Andrea laughed and giggled as Tim kissed all over her. His lips tickled her earlobes, her neck, then he kissed down to her breasts. He took the left nipple into his mouth as Ella Mai's *Boo'd Up* came on.

Andrea's back arched. She moaned, hissing with bliss as she felt his tongue swirling around her nipple. His hands held her by her waist, keeping her close to him. Tim went to her right breast and pleasured her more, making her hotter by the second. He released it a minute later, and kissed his way down her flat stomach, stopping at her sweet-smelling womanhood.

He looked up at her and made eye contact since she was already looking at him. With a mischievous smile on his face, he lifted her up, surprising her, and carried her over to the bed and dropped her on it.

Tim stripped out of his clothes, slowly, seeing how turned on she was by his striptease. Andrea licked her lips as she drank in the sight of his toned muscular tattooed body. It was like looking at the world's most handsome gangster that only *she* could have. When he reached up to take his chain off, she stopped him. She loved the way the diamonds looked against his skin and it was a visual she wanted to keep.

Tim made his way back to her. He climbed onto the bed and parted her legs. He reached in and ripped a hole in her pantyhose. Diving his face in between, he smelled her flower. His mouth watered from her delicious scent.

Andrea shrieked with delight when he ripped her thong off with his teeth, exposing her shaved womanhood. He kissed her swollen lips then ran his tongue up the slit, slurping her juices that leaked.

She shuddered at the feeling of his tongue and lips kissing her southern lips. She grabbed and started to caress her own breasts, adding to her pleasure. With her eyes closed, she felt him pushing the hood of her clit up, then a second later, she felt him take her clit into her mouth.

"*Oooooo*, Tim! *Oohhh!*" Andrea cried out, back arching as Megan Thee Stallion's *Don't Stop* featuring Lil' Baby came on.

Tim sucked her clit, making her gush like a geyser. Her head spun around as he went in on her. It had been so long since she had any intimate time with a man and, as far as she could remember, every single sexual encounter she had experience was *way* less than pleasurable.

He had her going crazy and she leaked like a broken faucet. He drank her up, savoring her taste and kept going. A few minutes into his oral torture, Tim inserted two fingers inside of her and slightly curled them. When he started stroking her, his curled fingers stimulated her sensitive walls, making her crave penetration.

Andrea screamed out at the tops of her lungs as she arched up off the bed and looked damn near like a spider, unable to handle such bliss. She plopped back down a minute later, then she exploded, squirting Tim right in his face.

"Fuck!" she cursed, laying limp on the bed, chest rising and falling rapidly, as she tried to catch her breath. "Wow... wow... *Wooow*!"

Tim started laughing. Her reaction told him that he had just did what no other man had ever did before, at least not to her satisfaction. He was ready to slide up in it and pound the pussy, but Andrea had the mindset to reciprocate whatever was done for her. So, she pushed him over onto his back, got up on her knees next to him, hunching over. She took his throbbing hardness into her hand and lowered her head down until her lips touched it.

Tim smiled like a kid in the candy store when he watched her perky lips kissing on his shaft, making their way up to the bulbous tip. She took him into her hand, held it up right then she opened her mouth wide and engulfed him, going balls deep. He felt his dick reach the back of her throat as she closed her mouth, wrapping her lips tightly around him. He groaned as she sucked, slowly making her way up to the tip, while she made her tongue swirl around his member on the way up.

"Shit, baby! Damn, that feels good," he told her, knowing that most women wanted to *hear* that they were doing a good job.

Andrea went back down, her lips touching the base of his cock. She started humming, a trick she had learned on *PornHub*, and Tim jumped when he felt the deep vibration tickling his loins.

"Whoa!" he shouted, toes curling up so hard that he thought that they might break off.

Andrea found even more pleasure in the fact that she was making him feel good. She had secretly been playing out how she would make him want her since she had met him. In no way, shape, or form did she feel like a slut for getting down like she was with him the same day that she met him. She felt a connection with him and the way he looked at her, plus going through what they had just gone through together, they already had a bond that was like no other.

All that was left was to share the intimacy of joining their bodies and spirits, and Andrea had *every* intention of making it a night to remember. She started going crazy, sucking fast, moaning, making it loud and sloppy. Tim was groaning and cursing, squirming, and his face was contorting like he was a shapeshifter. She felt him reach around her to palm her ass and rub on it through her ripped pantyhose. He played with her wet pussy from the back, then with his middle finger wet, he stuck it into her asshole and started finger-fucking it.

Andrea tooted it up higher for him, encouraging him to get nastier, to put it all the way in. Tim's eyes rolled to the back of his head while his finger went in and out of her brown eye faster and faster. He felt his nut rising quickly and she could taste his pre-cum while his dick was pulsating in her throat. She removed her hands but continued to suck him up until he bust.

"Woooo!" Tim shouted as he came so hard that he felt it in his spine.

Andrea made sure that she didn't miss a drop as she continued to suck. Once she swallowed she wiped her mouth, feeling satisfied with her performance.

"*Mmmmm!* Tasty," she purred, rising back up on her knees, looking at him with the sexiest seductive face that Tim had ever seen.

"Wow… holy shit… you got skills," Tim said, damn near speechless from how bomb the head was.

"You think *that* was good, huh?" she asked. "You ain't felt shit yet, handsome."

She climbed on top of him, right as the song changed to Jeremih's *I Like* featuring Ludacris. Grabbing his still hard dick, she positioned herself over it, then lowered herself down until all of him was inside of her.

"Oohhh, my muthafuckin' *God!*" he exclaimed, eyes rolling to the back of his head when he felt how tight, warm, and wet she was.

She felt like she was made for him. Like the pussy had never been touched, waiting for him to be the one to bust it open and christen it, plant his flag on her and claim her as his.

Andrea started riding him, hands on his chest, eyes on his, her heart beating with his. She made love to him with more than her body. She made love to his soul as well.

Tim was so baffled by the angelic Italian beauty that was on top of him that all the other women that he had smashed instantly faded from his mind. He couldn't remember a single one of their names, and he didn't care to either.

She climaxed all over him nearly ten minutes later. They switched; she was put on her side, Tim behind her, holding her leg up while he fucked her on his side, murdering the pussy and making her scream his name, begging for him to not stop.

She exploded on him again. Tim made her ride him reverse-cowgirl style and watched her ass bounce up and down while she used his dick to fuck herself to another orgasm.

After that, he got her on her hands and knees, face down, ass up. He leaned his face down and put it between her sweaty ass cheeks, and ran his tongue up her crack, swirling his tongue around her puckered pink butthole. Andrea squealed into the bed sheets. Little did Tim know it, but she had never been anally pleasured before. It was new to her and made her feel so dirty and nasty in the best way.

Tim lifted, scooted close, and slid himself inside of her. The Dream's *Falsetto* came on. Andrea cried out, matching the cries of the song as Tim cracked her from behind. He gripped her ass cheeks, sticking a finger in her asshole. Andrea screamed and cried out his name, damn near seeing stars.

Tim kept his stroke game strong until she climaxed again all over his thighs. He pulled his dick out of her pussy and slipped it into her back door, stretching her all the way out. Andrea relaxed her anal tract, inviting him to truly dominate her. Feeling his dick in her asshole made her feel like she was his, that he had made her his, and she loved the feeling.

Minutes later Tim started cursing and groaning, feeling his nut ready to bust. His dick swelled inside of her. She felt it and reached back so she could pull him out of her. With his dick in hand, she told him to stand up in front of her and adjusted her body so she was facing his hard member.

Tim stuffed his cock back into her mouth and fucked her face until he came. He filled her mouth up again with his essence and she sucked it all out of him and let it dribble down onto her chest, smiling up at him with the naughtiest look on her face.

"Okay. You just proved your point, baby," Tim said to her, sweating and breathing hard.

He reached down to pull her up from the floor.

"I aim to please, especially when I'm making it a point to establish myself as the one you need in your life," she told him, looking directly up into his eyes.

"So, you're tellin' me you're tryna be mines?" he asked. "Even with the fact that we just met today?"

"We just had the dirtiest kinkiest sex, like we've been dating for more than a year. I think that factor has gone right out of the window, Tim."

Tim busted out laughing. "Well, when you put it like that," he said, as SZA's *Hit Different* featuring Ty Dolla $ign came on.

She smiled up at him before reaching around him and wrapped her arms around his waist.

"You still upset over your car?" she then asked him, gazing into his dreamy eyes.

"Fuck that car; as long as you cool, then I'm cool," Tim replied, with a gigantic grin on his face.

"Aww! Tim, you are so sweet! But I don't think I'm worth a destroyed Ferrari."

"Nope. You're not, gorgeous; you're worth more," Tim told her. "Now lemme' show you how much you are worth to *me*."

Andrea then screamed excitedly when Tim scooped her up and tossed her all the way over to the bed. She bounced up and down on it, then he ran and catapulted himself up into the air, slam dunking himself on top of her, ready for round 2, 3, 4, *and* 5, just like she was.

Chapter 14

Two weeks later

Early one morning, just after 7 o'clock, Tracy showed up to baby sit Eric Jr. and Monique. With her were her four Blue-nosed killers; Stripes, Mongo, Moose, and Shark. LaLa and Deuce dwarfed the Razor Edge line Pits. The four ran to them, excitedly jumping around their much bigger companions.

Tracy had brought a bag of cash that had come from the coke and dope that Bunz had hit her with the previous day. Drugs placed in Tracy's hands turned into cash faster than McDonald's sold hot cakes.

Bunz took a shower and dressed in a black silk Versace shirt with gold and blue designs all over it, a shiny gold leather mini skirt, and blue and gold Versace stilettos on her feet that had blue ankle ribbon ties.

She pulled her locs up into a ball atop her head, applied a little makeup, then she draped herself in gold Tiffany & Co jewelry, spritzing on some Versace perfume when she was all finished getting sexy for the day.

Sonia had ordered herself some clothes to be delivered. Once they came, she got showered and dressed in the bubble-gum-pink Chanel ankle-length dress that fit her body like a second skin and had slits up both sides that went up to her upper thighs. Its low cleavage line gave off ample view of the tops of her perky breasts, and the long sleeves were a see-through pink style. The designer's iconic double C's were all over the dress in white letters; on her feet, she put on pink Chanel pointed-toe pumps with white belt-like ankle-straps.

She put her hair up into a high ponytail, styled her baby hair edges to emphasize her remarkably beautiful face. Pink eyeshadow, glossy pink lipstick, went with the white double-c Chanel earrings she put on, the matching necklace, rings, and bracelets. Last, after she donned her new white ceramic and diamond Chanel J12 watch, she put on some Chanel perfume.

Tracy had brought her favorite cookbook with her. She claimed the famous basketball wife of Ayesha Curry, as her food hero. Her recipe book, *The Seasoned Life*, sat opened on the counter. Tracy had all the ingredients she needed already in Bunz's kitchen, as she often cooked whenever she came over. The book that the African American, Jamaican, Chinese, and Polish chef created was opened to the page for her PB&J French Toast, that would have crushed Frosted Flakes added in the bowl of egg-wash for the thick slices to be dunked in and fried up on in a skillet.

While she got to it, Bunz sat at the table with Sonia and the babies in their baby chairs. Numerous deposits had been made into Bunz's personal and business accounts. All the legitimate businesses that she and Eric had owned were still going very strong.

Other types of electronic deposits went into her untraceable account, all coming from the tops of each of her crews flooding the streets of northern Illinois with cocaine, heroin, ice, pills, and fentanyl.

Bunz looked at the deposit made by the supervisor of the world class weight-lifting gym that she had bought and created for Eric. The amount was staggering. Many people were joining the gym. It made her think that Planet Fitness and Gold's Gym might have some competition, if she were to choose to open more locations.

She saw the profits that came from the indoor dog exercise park. Nobody anywhere in the world, that she knew of, had built what was so very much like the great outdoors for dogs, inside of a building. It proved to be perfect for those that wanted to play with their dogs somewhere else, even if the weather was bad, or if dogs had certain allergies that acted up when they got too close to certain plants or anything else that would be in an outdoor dog walk park. She had been thinking of adding a small dog restaurant inside that served treats and food for dogs, as well as traditional human foods and deserts.

Having been taught by Eric to share the wealth, while Tracy started frying up slices of French toast, Bunz went and made massive anonymous donations to charities that focused on hungry African families, underprivileged kids in America, and to organizations that helped kids with cancer or other deadly ailments and disorders live as long as they possibly could. She would want someone to do the same thing for *her* children, if they had the means to do so.

***

Andrea giggled her ass off as Tim kissed and sucked on her neck, while his hands squeezed on her ass.

"Tiiiiim! Come on, you horn-ball," she playfully whined, though she really did not want him to stop.

She was dressed in a retro 80's looking Rag & Bone outfit that consisted of a bright neon green long-sleeved belly shirt that was under an acid-washed denim vest and a tight skinny-leg acid-washed denim jeans, and on her feet were pink, Red Bottom sneakers with spike studded toes. Her hair had been styled up into a bun that rested on the top of her head, and she wore pink lipstick, with white-gold hoop earrings in her ears and a white-gold rope chain around her neck.

Tim had dressed in the Gucci fit that he had delivered to the house. The white t-shirt had a patch of Gucci designs across the chest; the shorts that went with it were beige and monogrammed with Gucci G's, and they matched the low-top sneakers on his feet. Gucci shades framed his handsome face. A gold Gucci watch was on his wrist, and flawless diamond studs flicked in his ears like the ones in his long gold Cuban link chain.

"I can't help it. You got a nigga straight feenin' for this ass right now, 'Drea. Goddamn this muhfucka soft," he said, raising her skirt up and squeezing her bare booty cheeks that swallowed up the tiny thong she had on.

"Tim, we can get naughty again after I get my license. Right now, we gotta get to the DMV for my appointment," Andrea told him, trying so hard to maintain control of herself.

"Okay. Let's gon' 'n get up outta here, future driver girl. Oh, by the way, I think Bunz has somethin' for you, too."

Andrea's eyebrows furrowed as her took her by the hand and led her out of her loft to the house, where the mouth-watering aromas of someone that knew what they were doing wafted into their nostrils.

They got to the kitchen and saw stacks of French toast on a plate, with sausage links, turkey bacon, hash browns, and sliced fruit. Tracy was just finishing up with the last of the food while Bunz and Sonia were sitting at the table, playing with the twins, while the dogs were laid out by the glass door to the backyard, bathing in sunlight.

Bunz looked at Andrea and smiled. She held up a key fob, gesturing her to come grab them. Andrea went to get them and saw the *Land Rover* emblem on them.

"Enjoy your new ride while you get your license," Bunz told her.

Andrea gasped in shock. "Holy shit! You... you're giving me... a whip?!"

"Yep. It's in the fourth garage bay. Take it to your exam and I bet money you'll pass the drivin' part *easily*," Bunz told her.

Saying bye to the babies and the dogs, then to Bunz, Tracy, and Sonia, Andrea nearly yanked Tim out of the house with her to the garage.

***

Barely able to contain herself, Andrea did all she could to keep from jumping up and down as the bay door rolled up. Tim could see how excited she was. He knew he would be too, if his first vehicle would've been a Range Rover, and not a '85 Ford Mustang 5.0.

Andrea squealed in delight when she saw the *Overfinch* edition inside the port. She was surprised that she had not seen it before, since she lived on the garage's loft.

The *Satin Silver Ice* paint looked made the SUV look so clean and classy at the same time. The custom carbon-fiber body styling, the carbon-fiber roof and spoiler, the black accents made it stand out from so many others. Even the blacked-out Overfinch exhaust pipes were engraved with the designer's emblem. It sat on 23-inch, 2-tone machined-silver and black Overfinch rims, wrapped in high-performance tires that gripped asphalt like a Pit Bull did a burglar.

"Now that is definitely a dope-ass whip," Tim had to admit, as they stepped inside the port and got a good look at black and silver interior.

"My first vehicle is a Range Rover… this is crazy," Andrea shook her head, astounded at her own words.

Just a few days ago, she was a new part-time chef at a prestigious restaurant, that she wasn't even sure how she got hired at, living in a shelter for abused women and kids, and she had absolutely no money. Now, she was caked up, had some of the most exclusive designer swag a woman could want, jewelry, a fly-ass residence, a $200,000 dollar SUV, sitting on some seriously nice rims, and she had an outrageously handsome dude that was caked up, and could make her cum harder and more times than any other man had ever done in her life.

"Good things come to those that deserve it," Tim told her, opening the driver's door for her.

Andrea let him take her hand and help her up behind the wheel. He closed the door and went to hop in with her. Andrea push-started the engine. She got goose bumps from the sound of the powerful supercharged V8 engine's purr.

Putting it in reverse, she backed out of the garage, then about faced, pulling off and glancing at the house as she passed it, geeked to be going to get her license so she could drive her new truck legitimately like a boss.

***

Paula brooded hard, irate that the multiple attempts on her life, in the course of an hour, had been made. Her man's head had been sliced off, his body left on the ground at the club, now it was all over the biggest news channels in Wisconsin.

Sitting on the bed in a hospital room, she sighed to herself. The door opened and in came her uncle Donnie, her uncle Vince, her aunt Angela, and her big brutishly build cousins Marco, Frankie, Leonardo, and Tony. Paula's eyes went wide with shock when she saw them. They lived in Calabasas, where her father was killed by that diamond-snatching bitch.

What in the hell are they doing here in Wisconsin? she asked herself, as Donnie and his wife marched up to her side, with Vince next to his older brother.

"Paula! What in God's name were you thinking?!" Donnie demanded to know.

He was the oldest of them all. He was big, round, and balding up top. He didn't look like much, but Donnie was a *made* man in the Italian mafia's Los Angeles faction. His brother was made, and Angela was heavy in the mob as well. Paula's cousins were soon to become part of it; for years, since they were in their teens, they had been putting in work and had quite the reputation as bone crushers. "Rubio is dead! You were supposed to come back to Calabasas and let *us* handle that twit, goddammit!"

Donnie was even angrier about Rubio's death; he had been grooming Rubio to become official, under his wing.

"And you involved the cops in what should have been left to us to handle," Vince added, giving her a look of disdain.

"You know better than that, Paula," came Angela, looking at her niece with disapproval. "Your father's probably rolling over in his grave right now."

Paula's cousins stayed quiet during the verbal lashings that their youngest cousin was getting from the old heads. Paula, though, couldn't take it. She exploded with anger.

"Do you *really* think I've done worse than what my *fucking* father did?" she shot back at them.

"Hey! You watch your mouth, young lady!" Angela scolded.

"Fuck that! My father got killed over some fucking pussy! My fucking mother died because of his stupid ass mistakes!" Paula raged at the men in front of her.

Donnie, Vince, and Angela slowed their role. They knew Paula was a hot head, but they also knew that she was right. Barry, having indulged in the same guilty pleasures that got so many other men, and women, robbed and killed, or locked up, was what ultimately led to his demise, and the demise of his wife.

"Alright." Donnie took the hand of his oldest brother's daughter and held it. "I understand. But from this point on, let *us* handle this, okay, sweetheart."

Paula looked him in his eyes, then she gave him a faint nod.

"Now you say it's the bitch that killed Barry that did this?" he asked her.

"I'd bet my life it's her, Uncle Donnie. I can feel it in my bones."

"Then we're gonna go find that little cunt and have a long painful chat with her," Angela chimed in, "and after that chat, I'm gonna break every bone in her body, then I'll shackle her to cement blocks and drop her into Lake Michigan so she can sleep with the fishes."

Old school… get it right, you old bitch, Paula thought to herself.

"For now, we'll be in the hotel around the corner from here; when you get discharged, we'll take you back home to California with us, and we'll have the cunt taken and brought to us," Vince told his niece.

Donnie, Vince, and Angela kissed Paula on her forehead, then they left out to make some calls. Marco, Frankie, Leonardo, and Tony all stayed in the room with her. Marco, the oldest, went and closed the door. Then he and his line-backer-size brothers went to Paula's bed side.

"We know you're not gonna let the old geezers take care of it themselves," Marco said, knowing that his baby cousin was the most rebellious person on earth.

Paula started grinning her ass off. "Not a snowball's chance in hell would I let *them* get the bitch before *me*. Who the fuck does cement shoes anymore these days?"

Her cousins laughed.

"The bitch is mine; I know how to get her."

"Well, don't keep us in suspense," Frankie said. "Cut us in or cut it out."

"Yeah, punk," Leonardo told her.

Tony chuckled.

Paula ran down her thoughts on how she could catch the elusive Bunz and kill her, for real this time. Her cousins listened intently, smiles growing on their faces that resembled devious plots inside of their heads. They all had the same goal by the end of her plan.

Kill the bitch, anyone that was with her, and take back what she stole.

Chapter 15

Bunz pushed her black-on-black Bentley Mulsanne Speed Premiere south down I-94 to Illinois, nodding her head to Saweetie's *Back to the Future* featuring Jhenè Aiko as it bumped from the four 10-inch subwoofers in the trunk. Sonia silently mouthed the words to the chorus, leaned back in the passenger's side.

Soon after reaching the end of Pleasant Prairie, at the Wisconsin-Illinois state line, Bunz got off the highway at Russell Road, shot down to Frontage Road and made a right turn, going back north for a few minutes. Sonia saw that Bunz was about to make a left turn into her big commercial truck wash and detail business. She smiled to herself, liking how Bunz had seriously expanded her portfolio as a business owner, turning all that dirty money into clean currency.

Bunz turned into her lucrative truck stop business and passed by a row of trucks that had just gotten washed and were shining like they were brand new. She headed around the north side of the massive building which had a fueling station, a large amount of space for trucks to park and for their drivers to get some rest, and along with a small restaurant inside, showers, a laundry mat, and a convenience store combined all in one, and bent the corner.

Sonia saw a big rig parked alongside of the rear of the long indoor wash port structure. Her eyebrows rose when she saw how chromed out it was and took in the fancy custom emerald-green paint job.

"Damn. Bro be going *crazy* with all them fancy-ass trucks he got, girl," she said to Bunz, as Bunz pulled around the driver's side of the luxurious brand-spanking new Peterbilt 589, which was coupled to a fifty-three-foot long dry-van box trailer that had gleaming aluminum wheels and a paint job that matched the truck.

Bunz chuckled. "Macho, Tool, Yessy, Gabi; they all do that stuff to these big ass trucks," she said, parking at the side of the big inventory garage that the rig's trailer's rear end was a few feet in front of. "Javi 'n all them, too. They some straight up truck nuts."

She parked at the side door of the garage and killed the engine. She and Sonia hopped out and looked up towards where the custom suicide driver's door of the Peterbilt had just opened. First came a blue Timberland boot, followed by long glossy caramel-colored leg with a Puerto Rican flag tatted on the outer calf. The beautiful Nuyorican queen that had been behind the wheel then got out of the cab. The 5'9" belle was wearing a denim acid-washed mini-skirt and a white tank-top with Gucci in blue letters across her ample bosom. Her tatted arms and chest were on full display. Her long, silky, light blue tinted hair flowed in the light gusts of wind that flew past her as her feet hit the ground. Her all blue ensemble matched the ridiculously expensive blue diamond that was mounted on a pure platinum band, put on her finger by her billionaire cocaine drug lord husband a few years ago.

Bunz and Sonia screamed with excitement when they saw the voluptuous Gina Rodriguez clone. Yessy herself screamed excitedly, running to meet them halfway by the rear wheels of the fancy tractor.

"Giiirl, look at you! Hoppin' outta this big-ass thang rockin' a tiny-ass skirt 'n shit! Yo' husband know about you comin' out here lookin' like this?" Bunz asked her, as she and Sonia both hugged Yessy.

"Girl, I am a grown-ass woman, and I'm a married. My hubby ain't got shit to worry about if I pop out lookin' like

I'm about to go shake my ass, or go to work, 'nah mean, B?" the south Bronx-born Nuyorican said with a grin and a strong New York accent.

From around the truck's front end, Yessy's best friend of more than fifteen years came around, looking just as good and thick as hell. Her skin was the color of maple pancake syrup and she too was dressed in a fresh white Gucci tank-top that let her tatted arms, buxom chest, and the short purple and blue leather mini-skirt she had on hugged her plump round ass and let her thick oiled tattooed legs and thighs to show. On her feet were the very rare and expensive sold-out Christian Dior edition Air Jordan 1s on her feet, and her long dark brown hair braided intricately, tied up and hanging down the right side of her shoulder.

"Gabrielaa!" sang Sonia, geeked to see the 5'8", Chicago-born, Boricua.

G-Baby, as she was called, had a gigantic smile on her face as she was also greeted emphatically by Bunz and Sonia. The two loved the Puerto Rican belles like sisters. Sonia had known them for a significantly longer time than Bunz had, but quickly, Bunz had become like their little sister.

Yessy and G-Baby were two of the most beautiful women that Bunz had even had the pleasure to meet in person. Women like them only existed in Urban novels or in high-action packed movies. They were fearless, and ruthless when it came to putting in work. They were both stupid rich, and extremely smart. They had resources and connections that made people's jaws drop, and the fact that they were both ex-military and grew up on the streets, not many people could hold a candle to them, whether it came to throwing hands, or tossing lead. The funny thing about the two, was that they both resembled famous actresses. Yessy had an uncanny resemblance to the Chicago-born Boricua Gina Rodriguez, while G-Baby favored the former *Chicago P.D.* Latina cop Vanessa Rojas, played by Lisseth Chavez.

"Oh, my God, G-Baby, you lost all that baby weight, girl!" Sonia exclaimed, unable to refrain from commenting on how the Humboldt Park gangstress looked good enough to hit the runway in Paris from how perfect her post-pregnancy figure was. "You look so good!"

"Why, thank you, sexy Persian girl," G-Baby replied, in the femininely raspy voice that made people think of the singer Keyshia Cole when she spoke. "When you live with this crazy bitch and our even crazier man, there ain't no such thing as bein' overweight."

Bunz and Sonia were still amazed by how Yessy was married to Macho, while G-Baby was his girlfriend. The three had the most incredible three-way relationship, and it worked. So many people coveted the love they had and the true friendship.

Chuckling, Bunz was about to lead the ladies to the door, when she heard the man of the hour's voice. She and the women turned and saw Macho climbing down from the truck, rocking a blue tank-top, denim shorts, with blue Timberlands on his feet. His long dreadlocks were roped into four barrels, hanging down past his broad muscular shoulders.

Antonio "*Macho*" Tomas Valdez was far from the normal big dog. He was the type that stayed in the trenches, even though he could afford to pay mobs of goons to handle getting opps handled easily. He was someone that Bunz truly respected. When she first met the Dominican-Puerto Rican mixed goon, it had been with Eric, and what she learned about Macho amazed her.

Born and raised in Pittsburgh, Pennsylvania, Macho, and his older brother, were the creators of the *Steel City Mafia*, a mob of just seven tried and true gangsters that moved so much cocaine that Pablo would seem mediocre to anyone else.

He was a *huge* man; 6'3", muscular like a body builder, with hypnotizing bluish-gray eyes and a razor-sharp hairline and beard. He had long dreadlocks that were freshly re-twisted at the roots and roped back into four neat barrels. At thirty-five years old, he still looked like the young and wild killer he was known to be. Macho was tatted up like Lil' Wayne and was so bulky that just looking at him was intimidating to most people.

As a major cocaine trafficker and distributor for the whole mid-west and the east coast, Macho had so much money that he literally gave millions of dollars, exotic cars, mansions, and all sort of ridiculously expensive things away, just because. He made it all back with every big shipment of cocaine he and his brother brought in from the Dominican Republic, delivering truckloads of it to their long list of clients. There were so many people that loved him because of how gracious he was, but there were also so many people that hated him, because he didn't follow anyone.

He was talking on the phone via the Bluetooth earpiece in his ear as he walked up. Heavily engaged in a business call, Macho hugged Bunz and Sonia then went to the rear of the trailer, entering the digital combination on the lock to open it up and prepare to unload Bunz's goodies.

Bunz opened the garage up and let everyone into the big storage space. It was suggested by Macho that she open her own truck stop, since trucking was big business, especially in the Midwest. His wife and his girlfriend, both certified real estate agents in residential and commercial properties amongst so many other things, had brought Bunz to the property, which was formerly a franchise chain truck stop that the owner had put up for sale to go into retirement.

Bunz made the man an offer he couldn't refuse, and in the five months she had owned it, she had already made her money back and was in the black.

Inside, Bunz hit the button to open the garage. Yessy and G-Baby then assisted their man as he handed them cardboard boxes labeled with cleaning chemicals that did not have cleaning chemicals inside of them. Thirty ten-pound boxes had been hand-bombed out of the trailer before Macho hopped out and closed the two swing doors back. He entered the garage and hit the button to close the door.

"Special delivery, lil' sis," Macho said, as Bunz and Sonia stacked the boxes on a wooden pallet, leaving three to the side, one for the salon, and one to take to one of the most profitable dope spots that Bunz had.

"Thank you kindly, bro'," Bunz said, giving him another hug. "How you all been doin', though? Everything good?"

"Yeah. Just miss E every day that we wake up, 'yah mean? My nigga gone and that bitch is alive. ¡A mi no me gusta esa 'mielda!" Macho snapped, saying he didn't like that shit.

"Que se vaya pa' carajo, esa mamabicho," *Let that bitch go to hell.* Yessy put her arm around her husband's waist. "The bitch will get got, yo. On my Romeo's grave."

Hearing Yessy's younger brother's name made Bunz's heart drop. She had never got the chance to meet the young gun, but she knew how close that Yessy and Romeo had been with each other. They came up from the mud, having really nobody but each other to depend on but themselves. Everyone was devastated when Yessy's brother was murdered, but what was even worse about that dark bloody day, was that G-Baby's younger sister had been killed as well when they were caught off guard and chased by a shooter, ultimately losing their lives in a fiery crash that resulted in closed-casket funerals.

Bunz nodded her head. She appreciated how much Macho, and his ladies were still bent up over Eric's death. At the end of the day, she knew that she had some real live goons that would walk alongside her through the gates of hell to fight Satan's army without any hesitation if she needed them to.

***

115

After the boxes loaded with Grade A cocaine, freshly imported into the states from the Dominican Republic, were taken down to the subterranean level of the storage garage and stashed, Bunz and Sonia hugged the three filthy rich Afro-Latino goons and bid them adieu. They hopped back into the Peterbilt, G-Baby behind the wheel this time.

Bunz and Sonia found themselves still so amazed that Yessy and G-Baby could drive such a big-ass truck. It roared out of the big, chromed exhaust pipes as G-Baby shifted gears, heading to exit the truck stop and head to their next drop-off spots.

"What could be better than ridin' around in a big semi?" Bunz asked aloud to Sonia, as she put the three boxes that she had kept with her into the secret trap spot in the trunk of her Mulsanne. "Droppin' off yayo by the truckload, pickin' up *tons* of cash, and havin' all the cops too damn afraid to pull you over because the reputation you have scares the living *shit* out of them?"

"Absolutely *nothing*," Sonia replied.

They hopped in and headed off. Bunz went and took the coke to the salon. Tanzanian was on point, wearing clothes, receiving the re-up and taking it right in to have broken down and cooked up.

Hopping back into the Bentley, Bunz and Sonia headed towards Zion to drop off one of the boxes of yayo to the dope house that Bunz had taken over for her deceased fiancé in the notorious Hebron apartment strip.

Coming down 21st Street in Zion, Bunz arrived at the alley way that ran through the Hebrons row building apartments. She made a right turn into the alley and saw many cars by Marcello's building, but no fiends, and nobody making serves.

"What the hell?" she said to herself, automatically alert to the situation, knowing that not even a single minute a day, did the Hebrons ever rest.

Even when cops rolled through, people continued doing them, daring the jakes to try them.

"Is something wrong?" asked Sonia, as Bunz went and parked next to Marcello's blacked-out Hellcat Charger.

"Yes. It's a ghost town out here; this isn't normal," Bunz told her.

She got her iPhone out and attempted to call Marcello. She got no answer. It went straight to voicemail. She tried once more but got the same result.

She muttered a curse under her breath. Grabbing her handbag, Bunz pulled out leather gloves, then after she put them on, she pulled out her two twin FN Five sevens out, both fitted with extended clips, each of them filled with 5.7x28 millimeter rounds that went through steel like it was butter. She cocked them and took the safeties off.

"Stay here," she told Sonia, right as she opened her door to get out.

"Not happening." Sonia reached into her own bag and got out her automatic Uzi and the 50-round stick, slapping it into the gun and cocking it. "I gave my word to Eric before he died, when he asked me to lure the bitch to y'all, to never ever let you go about some g-shit like what you are about to do, by yourself. I am *not* breaking that promise to my brother, Monique."

They both got out of the Bentley. Besides the cars rolling up and down 21st Street every so often, the Hebrons were eerily quiet. Bunz and Sonia looked around, looking for something that seemed out of place. They saw nothing, though.

Sonia gripped her Russian-spitter tightly in her hands and held it like she was an FBI agent, trying to sneak up on a dangerous criminal. Bunz's eyes shifted all around as they made their way to the cement passageway that led through the two buildings, where Marcello's spot was.

When they got there, Bunz stepped up onto the small cement porch. Sonia peeped through the window or tried to.

"The window is blocked with a blanket, Bunz," she whispered.

Now Bunz was sure that something was up. She had a feeling that as soon as she opened the door, she was going to get hit with a whiff of rotten meat. Sure enough, as Bunz opened the door, not at all surprised to discover that it wasn't even locked, the horrid odor of death smacked her right in her face and she almost vomited.

Sonia smelled it right away and gagged. "What the fuck?! Yo, like, for real?"

Bunz stepped inside and shook her head. The walls were covered with blood splatters. Bodies and body parts littered the blood-stained carpeted floor. She could tell that all the guys and the women inside were all the tenants of the apartments surrounding her dope spot, even though most of them were blown to pieces.

"Why is it that every time I come here, something seriously fucked up has happened?" she asked aloud, remembering having to come regulate in that trap spot before, in which Eric had showed up and blew the original leader's head off, and promoted Marcello to the boss spot.

Bunz looked and saw Marcello. His head was on the couch, his torso was on the floor, and his legs were on the ground.

"Has it ever been *this* fucked up?" Sonia asked, squeezing her nostrils closed while she looked around at the bloody massacre.

"Not even close. I bet everything that was worth money is gone," Bunz said.

"Unless whoever did this wasn't after dope or money," Sonia said to her, pointing to the wall to their left.

Bunz looked and saw, in bloody letters… KING LUV!

She shook her head. "Only one way to find out," Bunz replied, shaking her head at the bloody graffiti words. "Let's go see what's missin' from Marcello's safe."

"Great. I'm gonna smell like death by the time we get out of here. Whoever did this, I'ma shoot their dick off and stuff it up their own ass!"

Bunz laughed at her then they both went to go to where Marcello kept the stash.

Chapter 16

"Yes! Yes! Yes! Yeah, muthafucka I passed!" Andrea shouted excitedly, holding up her new license for Tim to see. "You see that? Yep, that's me! Woo-woo!"

Leaned up against her Range Rover Tim smiled, clapping his hands for her. She came towards him and was immediately wrapped up in his big arms. He kissed her lips when he pulled her closer to him, softly squeezing her ass.

"Congratulations, beautiful. I'm proud of you."

"Aww, gee thanks, babe," Andrea gushed, batting her eyelids at him.

"Care to go somewhere and celebrate?" Tim asked her.

"Uh-uh... Timothy!"

Andrea spun around when she heard some woman yelling. She saw a stunning woman, standing a few feet away from her, with her hands on her hips, looking irate. She was brown-skinned with long extension braids that were light brown and dark brown, and she was wearing a lavender-colored bra top, with denim booty shorts, and fresh white Air Force 1s on her feet.

Tim snaked his head around Bunz and saw his ex-jump off. He groaned with frustration.

"Not this bitch again man!" he said to himself, though Andrea heard him.

"And who exactly *is* this bitch, *Tim*?" she asked him, though she was eying the girl with a venomous glare.

"She is my crazy-ass ex."

The woman marched a few more footsteps towards them. Andrea could see the anger and the hurt in her eyes.

"This what you left me for, dude?! A white bitch?!" the girl snapped as she tried to go around Andrea and get up in Tim's face.

"I left you because you are too damn wild, Shaniqua," Tim told her, releasing and stepping around Andrea, getting in front of her, knowing that his ex-girlfriend loved to fight, anywhere.

"So what, Tim?" she snapped, getting all up on Tim, gritting her teeth.

Andrea narrowed her eyes. Her blood started boiling as she grew angrier and angrier that the bitch was straight up spazzing on her dude, out in the parking lot, ruining her moment of excitement.

Shaniqua turned her eyes from Tim and looked at Andrea. She clenched her teeth, enraged that a white girl had taken her place in Tim's heart, and in his pocket.

"You took what was mine, bitch! Why the fuck you don't go get a white boy?! Y'all white hoes *always* gotta go after *our* men!"

"Tim. Can I please have a word with this woman?" Andrea asked calmly.

"She is not worth fightin', 'Drea."

"Fightin'? Nigga that bitch don't want no smoke!" Shaniqua said, then started laughing, taunting Andrea.

"I'm not gonna fight her. I promise," said Andrea, then she stepped around him and stepped to Shaniqua, almost matching her in height, but was about a couple of inches shorter than her.

Shaniqua balled her fists up, ready to start swinging.

"Excuse me, Shaniqua?" Andrea said, closing the gap between them.

"Bitch, get the fuck out my face! I ain't got no rap!"

Andrea smiled, "Good."

CRACK! WHAM! BINK!

Tim's eyes went wide at how fast Andrea had just put the dukes on Shaniqua. He was 100% sure that *she* didn't realize what had happened, even after she hit the ground from the lightning fast three-punch combo. Andrea grabbed Shaniqua's head and delivered a devastating knee to her face, breaking her nose instantly.

Shaniqua screamed in pain as her nose gushed blood.

"Oh shit!" Tim gasped, wide eyed in shock. "What the fuck?"

Andrea stood there, looking down at the girl trying to hold her nostrils closed to stop the blood from flowing.

"You are the first woman to have *ever* did that to her," Tim told her.

"Hmmmm," Andrea hummed as she reached down and helped Shaniqua up. The girl leaned her head back, still squeezing her nose closed to stop the bleeding. "You shouldn't be so hostile towards people you can't handle. Being angry takes too much energy. Now run along to your car and go get your nose checked out, honey boo-boo."

Shaniqua shot a glance over to Tim. The malice in her eyes was obvious. He shook his head at her, choosing to stay silent. Turning on her Air Forces, she turned and started walking away, pissed.

Andrea then ran up behind her and kicked her right in her ass, spiking her. Shaniqua screamed when she felt the studs poke her.

"I said *run!* Dumb ass bitch," Andrea yelled.

Tim's eyebrows went wide, then he busted out laughing as Shaniqua ran, holding her ass as if she had to take a dump real bad. Off to the side, he heard laughter. He and Andrea turned and looked to see a group of young teens in a driver's education class had come out of the DMV building to watch. They were laughing their asses off at how Andrea had just treated the shit out of the girl.

"Now," Andrea said to Tim, rubbing his arms. "I have something I've been wanting to do for a while now, and working for Bunz, I am confident I can do it. But what would really assure me that I can do this, is a big strong sexy man with hypnotizing blue eyes and big-ass arms. Any chance you know someone like that that can help me?" she asked, with a mischievous smile on her face.

Tim nodded his head. "I do, in fact. This fly-ass nigga that got him a baaad-ass chick. The question is, what is required of this fly-ass nigga?"

"Hop in. I will show you," Andrea said, just as her phone started ringing.

She hurried to pull it out of her handbag and saw it was Bunz. She answered it and listened intently as Bunz spoke. Tim stood by and saw Andrea's eyes start narrowing.

"Say no more. We are down," Andrea said a minute later.

She ended the call and looked at Tim. "We have something to do for Bunz first, then we can go handle mines. You don't have a curfew, right?"

Tim busted out laughing at her. "Naw, baby. Haven't had one of those in a *very* long time."

***

Later That Night

"What up, fam? Ya'll still good?" asked the tall skinny dope fiend that had matted dreadlocks and tattered clothing and shoes.

Debo looked at him. "I am not doin' no mo' fronts, joe. You got some money?"

The others in Debo's crew were close by, serving clucks powder and crack-cocaine and heroin, laced with fentanyl. They were booming out of a house in Waukegan, right on Lennox, off what everybody in the Town called *The Set*. Fiends from all around Wauk-Town had heard about the quality of the product that Debo and his mob of Gangster Disciples and 4 Corner Hustlers had suddenly popped up with and flocked like hungry seagulls at a beach to get right.

"Maaaan, Debo, come on, famo! I get paid tomorrow, man! Don't do me like that," the fiend begged, itching for a hit of crack.

"Nigga it's gonna rain all day tomorrow," Debo snapped.

"So? What the fuck does that mean?"

"You work at an *outside carwash,* stupid!"

"Deeeboooo! *Please,* man! Just hit me wit' a 'fitty piece and I'ma put a c-note in yo' hands, fam! On *me!*"

Debo whistled loudly and caught the attention of some of his goons that were posted up by the curb, watching the block for any of Waukegan's not-so finest jump out boys and undercover narcotics cops, and the for the opposition.

"Aye! Y'all niggas come get this cluck ass clown up outta my face!" Debo yelled to them.

The fiend screamed in panic and took off running with the young goons giving chase.

Debo laughed his ass off, knowing that if they caught him, he would not be coming back. He looked at the whole block from off the porch of his crib. He was happy that he and his crew were eating again. For the longest, they had been losing so much money. All the fiends were going up to Zion to get their drugs. It had Debo pissed and ready to kick in whoever's door.

He knew exactly who was responsible for the flow of supreme product but what had him puzzled was the rumors that he had been killed. Still, though, his traps were pumping, and money was going to them, instead of to Debo's pockets. He was not for continuing to lose money, so Debo gathered a few of his guys and went to go do some scouting.

They found out where the main trap spot was. Seeing it was in the wild and crazy Hebron apartments, Debo knew that making a move there would likely never make him a suspect, to cops, or to the person that still had it juking. That night, he and his squad went up there, all in black, strapped up like they were going to war. Debo had a machete that he had been wanting to use after he had watched a cartel movie.

There had been a party popping off in the apartment that the trap was said to be in. Lying in the cut, Debo and his crew waited until it seemed like everyone who was a part of the trap was there, and inside, then they made their move.

They kicked the door in and got to dumping on everyone that was right there in the middle of the living room. The rest, they kept alive for a while, promising them if they gave up the goods, that they would not be hurt.

The guy that ran the spot refused and forbade anyone that remained alive with him to speak. Debo respected that the guy knew the game, and what could happen when one played. But still, business was business. They fanned the last of the guys down, leaving only one female alive, and the trap spot's top dog. They put a chopper to his head, demanding the girl to tell them where the merch was, or they would blow his brains out, then chop her up.

She gave the shit up right away as she pissed her pants. She told them where the drugs were, the cash, and even where Debo had a cache of guns and ammo. Then Debo sliced her head off, right in front of the trap boss.

Debo then went to take the machete to the guy. He tried to fight for his life, but when three of Debo's goons grabbed him and held him down, it was over with. Cutting him up and leaving him in the living room for whoever was the real boss to find, and get scared, Debo and his homies went to get the merch. Before they left, Debo got the idea to make the robbery look like it was someone far off from him, and his guys, Debo painted some gang-banging shit on the wall with one of the dead's blood. He chose to make it seem like the Latin Kings had done it, since they had been said to been kicking it lots of doors lately, and taking everything of value inside, while leaving nobody alive.

***

"Aye, Debo. I'm out, joe."

Debo saw one of the youngest hustlers on his team coming towards his porch, with a stack of cash to turn in for another pack. Everyone called him Meatball, since he was dark and round like one.

"Go get it from my bitch, she inside choppin' up," Debo told the youngster.

"Aight."

Meatball bypassed Debo and headed into the house to get his re-up. He entered and hollered out to Debo's girl.

"Aye, Ebony, I need another pack, shortie!"

Heading towards the kitchen where he knew Ebony cooked up crack, mixed up raw coke, and raw dope, he heard GloRilla's *Yeah Glo* blaring loudly.

Meatball stepped into the kitchen seconds later. He immediately froze in shock when he saw Ebony, sitting at the kitchen table, dead as fuck. She had the end of a cake-mixer beater jammed into her left eye, and her throat had been slit right open.

"*Oh shit!* Aye, Debo!" he called out.

Meatball ran up out of the kitchen, track-staring in his Jordans for the front door. He flew up out of the house, right as a black Lincoln Town car skidded to a stop where Debo stood by the street. He saw a big bulky light skinned guy hop out of the passenger's side, with two pistols in his hands.

"Nigga, what the fuck?!" Debo went to pull out his Glock as his young ones stopped pumping and rushed in his direction.

Before he could even raise his gun, the man that had hopped out of the Lincoln, that he initially thought was there to buy some loud, had hopped out with two semi-autos and ran up on him too fast for him to move out of the way. He swung one of the guns and bashed Debo right in his jaw, knocking him right on his ass.

BRRRRRRRRRRRRRRRRRRRRRRRRRRRRRRRRR!
BRRRRRRRRRRRRRRRRRRRRRRRRRRRRRRRRR!

Machine guns started going off. Debo heard his guys' screaming in agony, but he couldn't get up to help. His own gun had flown from his hand and wasn't anywhere close to him.

Suddenly, he was snatched up off the ground like he didn't weigh 205 pounds. He caught a glimpse of Meatball running out of the house and going to up his cannon, but unbeknownst to him someone in all black was hiding on the porch, right at the side of the front door, gripping a tomahawk hatchet in their hand.

***

"Debo! Aye, G," Meatball yelled in fear.

The second he stepped out onto the porch and saw Debo get his clock cleaned by the man that had jumped out of the Town car. Machine guns started booming and he looked and saw two beautiful women dumping from behind a parked car. They blew down Debo's guys like they were expert shooters.

Meatball went to draw his gun when out of nowhere, he felt a searing white-hot pain in his legs. Then the next thing he knew, he fell, but his legs remained standing. Blood spurted from the stumps where the hatchet sliced through them both just above his knees. Meatball was in such shock that he wasn't even able to understand what had happened.

He was stuck, staring upwards at the ceiling of the porch roof, when he saw a figure wearing all black with a hockey goalie mask appear over him, holding the bloody weapon.

***

Andrea hopped out from behind the wheel of the Lincoln and popped at one of the block boys attempting to shoot at Bunz. She hit him twice in his chest putting a stop to him where he stood, then one more slammed into his face, knocking his brains out of his head and splattering them on the window of the car he had been next to.

The shooting continued while Tim beat on Debo relentlessly with his pistols. Bunz and Sonia dumped at the others that failed miserably to come even close to hitting them. Andrea turned her head and saw Tracy on the porch, standing over Debo's young homie with her hatchet.

She watched as she raised the chopper up high, then the boy screamed, seconds before she brought it down as hard as she could on his face, literally splitting his wig in two.

Tim dragged the bloody Debo to the rear of the stolen Town car and Andrea hit the trunk button for him, then went to assist him tie the guy up by his ankles and his wrists, all while bullets flew in every direction.

Together, they hoisted him up and tossed him into the trunk. Andrea jumped back behind the wheel; Tim hopped in the front seat. Andrea mashed the gas and took off. Tim hung out of the window and dumped on two of Debo's goons that hopped up from next to his Charger, hitting them in their chests and stomachs, opening them up. Andrea blew past Bunz, and Sonia, reaching the end of the one-way street and bent the corner, making a clean get away with their target secured in the trunk.

Bunz and Sonia put the last three shooters out as Andrea and Tim made it up off Lennox. Tracy joined them with her bloody hatchet. They took off running, cutting through houses to where Bunz had parked her Bentley at the corner of McAllister and Cummings. Hopping in, Bunz hit the gas and rocketed off from her spot, dipping away from The Set, just as swarms of Waukegan Police cars came flying towards the bloody scene.

Chapter 17

"Ooohh yeeeaaah!" he groaned, holding onto her wide hips, as he thrust in and out of her. "You like that, Bunz? Huh? Tell me you like how my cock feels in your ass!"

"Mmmmm, I love it, Barry!" she capped, ready for him to bust his nut. Then he could go do what he always did after she let him fuck her in her ass, and she could make the move she'd been planning for the last two years happen.

"Fuck my ass, baby! Fuck my ass like it's all yours, and only yours!"

She put on a show for him, faking her pleasure, hyping his head up to make him feel like he was the man. Barry reached out and grabbed her silky long brown hair and wrapped it around his hand. He gave her all that he had, which had no real effect on her. In minutes, he started grunting and cursing, feeling his nut rising. His eyes rolled to the back of his head as he groaned gutturally.

Bunz could tell he was getting close. She could feel his dick spasming inside of her ass so she reached her right hand back and pulled his dick out of her. Barry stroked his cock while she held her juicy 46 inch ass open for him.

Seconds later, he came. He roared animalistically as he skeeted globs of hot cum all over her asshole. Barry howled as he emptied himself. Bunz felt all the hot droplets splattering in her crevice, filling it up. Once he was done, she waited, knowing the last thing he loved to do after he busted his nut, was coming.

Barry dropped down to his knees and fulfilled his sick-ass fantasy; he started slurping up his own cum out of her crack. He licked her clean and swallowed every last drop. Curling her lip up in disgust, Bunz continued to act like it was a turn on for her, even if the shit was nasty. Barry had long money, and money was her motive.

"God, I love this great big ass! It really reminds me of glazed Honey Buns! That's how you got your name, isn't it, Shannell?" he asked, calling her by what she had told him was her government name.

"Uh huh," she said, hiding her smirk, detesting the lame-ass dude with a passion.

Barry smacked her ass and kneaded it like it was cookie dough. He was infatuated with the size and shape of it. Bunz giggled and raised herself up from his desk. Turning to him, she smiled up at him, looking him in his eyes, seeing the sparkle inside of his.

"I think we should get back to your party now, Barry. Your wife and daughter are probably wondering where daddy dearest has gone. What do you think they'll do if they find out that your so-called 'business partner' is really your whore?"

Barry waved that off. "I run this house, Shannell. Me. When I'm with you, I don't give a fuck about anyone else. Let me go use the bathroom really fast," he told her, then he hurried off towards where the private bathroom in his of the grand 20,000-sqaure-foot Victorian mansion he owned. Slipping inside, Barry shut the door and locked it.

Bunz counted down from five, then she hopped to it. It was the moment she had been waiting for to come, for so long. She hurried to pull her silk panties and black pantyhose up from around her ankles. She fixed the little red wool skirt that went with the red business suit that made her look worthy of standing next to Kamala Harris.

Listening, she could hear Barry snorting inside of the bathroom. She knew he was powdering his nose as usual. He was a certified cokehead so she knew she had at least 7 minutes before he came out.

Okay! Here we go! she thought to herself, nervous as hell, but ready to make everything she'd done with the old bastard for the last two years well worth the embarrassment.

Over in the corner of Barry's office, a Picasso was hung on the wall. Bunz quick-stepped over to it and gently lifted it off the hook. She set it down on the suede button-tuck couch that it'd been hanging over, then looked back at the bathroom once more. She could still hear snorting, followed by grunting and groaning. After a second of silence, she heard a sneeze, then a curse before more snorting started up.

Turning back to the wall, an old school safe with a combination lock was hidden behind where the painting had been. Bunz had seen him enter the combination so many times that she could recite it in her sleep, but she had never been left alone in his office. She hurried to enter the combination, turning the dial to each number. Just under ten seconds later, the safe was unlocked. YES! she screamed inside, as she was just moments away from the biggest score ever.

Opening the safe, she saw it, around the neck of a plastic mannequin inside, gleaming brightly, even in a dark space. She gasped in awe of the big vintage white-gold necklace, embedded with flawless VVS diamonds. They hypnotized her with their glimmering shine. Bunz was so entranced by the priceless jewelry that she had stopped paying attention to anything else.

"Well, well, well, what a surprise."

Bunz shrieked when she heard Barry's voice behind her. She spun around and saw him, just a few feet away. In his hand was a 9- millimeter Sig Sauer. Bunz looked at the gun then at him.

"Going to try and steal from me?" he said to her, taking a step in her direction. "I knew you were a thieving little slut! You've been sucking and fucking me for the last two

years; you left your boyfriend to come be my bitch! Now I'ma gonna do away with you for good!"

Bunz screamed. "Barry, waaiitt!"

BOCKA BOCKA BOCKA BOCKA BOCKA!

***

Bunz shot up out of her sleep, drenched in cold sweat. Instinctively, she grabbed the Glock 21 that was under her pillow and pointed it straight ahead but nobody was there.

Her eyes focused in, the images of Barry coming so close to killing her fading away, resuming reality. She took a deep breath, trying to calm her rapidly beating heart. Her eyes started filling with tears as she lowered her gun to her side. She felt so alone without Eric. She had PTSD like a war veteran. All the things she had been through, Eric helped her through it to the point that she didn't need sleep meds of melatonin to help her rest peacefully.

She needed him. She didn't have him though, and it was really killing her, more and more every single day that passed.

***

Cassie giggled as her boyfriend rubbed and smacked on her ass inside of the auto restoration garage that he had been working in for over five years. He grabbed her perky little booty and hoisted her up, sitting her onto the hood of the bronze and gold-flaked Pontiac Firebird that he had been working restoring as his own personal project.

In the late-night hours, he had been the only one still in the shop. When he got the text from his woman that she was outside, a big smile grew on his face. There was only one reason that she came to his job when he was working late.

He opened the main door and saw his petite 5'4" girlfriend wearing a tight pink dress, sexy heels, and she had on some makeup, with her hair did up. He took one look at her and yanked her inside, closing and locking the door, kissing all over her, rubbing all over her athletically fit body, ready to put the dick to her and make cum all over the hood of his car.

"Oh, my God, Mark you are such a freak, babe," Cassie said, as he started pushing her dress up and exposing that she had on no panties of any kind.

He looked from between her legs, up to her face, to see her smiling mischievously. "Says the girl that comes here in a tight dress, heels, and isn't wearing panties," he said, with a mischievous smile of his own.

She smacked her lips. "Whatever, dude. Just shut your face and eat this pussy so I can wet your face. And after that I want you to bend me over the hood and fuck the shit out of my ass."

"Ooooo, I can definitely do that," he said with eagerness, then was about to dive down between her legs to get to pleasing her, when suddenly, one of the glass windows to the garage door exploded.

Mark and Cassie both jumped out of their skin from the suddenness of it. They looked and saw a brick had been thrown through the window.

"What the hell, dude?" Mark said, leaving Cassie on the hood of the Firebird and going to investigate.

Cassie slid down and followed, never having been the type to like being left alone. Mark looked out of the broken window and immediately saw red when his eyes landed on his ex-girlfriend standing outside, about fifteen feet or so away from the garage door, next to a Range Rover sitting on big custom rims.

"This fucking bitch! Is she outta her mind?!" he said to himself, seething in anger.

"Who is it, babe? Cassie asked, with furrowed eyebrows.

"Fucking Andrea! I'm gonna *kill* that bitch this time! Move outta my way!" he demanded, then pushed past her, running for the exit to go get her.

He pushed the door open and went to rush out, when the first step he took out of the garage, a bucket of old motor oil was thrown right into his face.

"Aaahhh! *What the fuck?*" he shouted, blinded by the thick globby liquid.

"Maark? Baby!" he heard Cassie yell.

Then suddenly, Mark heard Cassie scream, "Get off me, you stupid bitch!" right before he heard a loud *SMACK*.

After that, he heard a thump, then silence.

"Cassie! Baby, what happened?" he shouted, trying his damnedest to get the oil out of his eyes so he could see.

Then he heard his ex-girlfriend's voice, very close to him.

"The bitch is taking a nap, you punk-bitch he-man-woman beater," Mark heard her say, then…

CRACK!

A blunt object rocked him in the side of his head, sending him to the ground, face first, unable to move. He groaned in pain as his head throbbed. He still couldn't see. But he could hear.

"I bet you thought you would never hear from me again, huh? You dickhead bitch," Andrea asked, looking down at her abusive ex-boyfriend, as he writhed in pain on the ground, face slick with the old worn engine oil that Tim had thrown in his face, before smacking the shit out of the chick he was with hard enough to knock her out.

"Wh-What do you want, Andrea?!" Mark stammered, still trying to get the oil out of his eyes.

"I want you to feel how *I* felt when I thought I was in love with a man, until I found out I was stuck with a woman-hating *bitch*," Andrea told him, seething in anger as all the horrible days and nights of him putting his hands on her filled her mind.

Tim grabbed Mark by his long buckwheat colored hair and dragged him towards the entrance door of the garage, kicking and screaming. Andrea went and grabbed Cassie by her hair and dragged her right behind. They took the two inside of the garage, shut the door, and locked it, having no plans to emerge from it until Andrea had gotten her revenge from all the heartache and physical pain the Mark had plagued her with for *way* too long.

Mark couldn't see a damn thing, but he could hear the muffled cries of his chick. His hands had been tied behind his back, and he was lying face up on the ground from what he could tell.

"Please, Andrea! Please! I'm sorry! I left you alone, goddammit! Let's just let the past be the past!" Mark begged.

WHAM!

A foot kicked him in the side of his head. Mark yelped in pain.

"Shut cho' bitch ass up, hoe-ass cracker! Don't nobody give a fuck about them pleas you tryna kick to us!" he heard the guy his ex-girlfriend was with say. "You wanna lay yo' hands on a woman, we gon' flip the script on it and let you see how bad you fucked up!"

The scarf was untied from around his face. His vision was blurry, but he could see better. The lights had been turned on, illuminating the entire garage. He saw Cassie tied up and laying on a mechanic crawler. Hanging over her was a 350 cubic-inch V8 engine, held suspended in the air by a thick chain that was a part of an engine hoist's hydraulic lifting system.

"Wait! Hold on! She didn't do anything," Mark said, pleading for Cassie's life.

He saw Andrea, standing next to the lever that would ultimately drop the engine, and crush her to death.

"She didn't have to do anything. *You* did, bitch!" Andrea said. "*But*," she added, "I'm not like you; I don't believe that she should die because you're a bitch. Sooooo…"

Andrea reached down and yanked Cassie from under the engine. Mark then felt himself being dragged over to take her place.

"Oh God, no! Noo! Andrea!" he cried, so scared that he started pissing his pants. "I'm sorry, I'm sorry, I'm so sorry!"

"You're sorry, Mark?" she asked, looking down at him, directly into his eyes.

"*Yes! I'm sorry!* I'm so sorry! I was a jerk and you didn't deserve it but please … *don't kill me!*"

Andrea smiled at him then. "I have been waiting for an apology for a very long time. I gotta be honest; I never thought you would ever speak those words, Mark."

He looked up at her, hoping to God that she believed him. The engine hanging over him would give him no chance at survival if it was dropped.

"I should have sought you out a long time ago, Andrea. For real, baby. I'm a changed man now. I have been trying to be a good man to Cassie; she changed me for the better. I swear to you."

He saw Andrea nod her head. Her face went from angry to neutral. He was filled with relief as it began to look like he might make it out of there alive.

"Okay. So, this is what's going to happen, Mark," Andrea said.

He watched her walk over to a metal worktable and picked up a tire iron, then came back to him. Mark instantly started panicking again.

"W-W-What are you gonna do with that?! I apologized to you, Andrea!"

"I know. I know. I'm not gonna kill you. You manned up and apologized, but for all those times you hit me, I *got* to break something," she said, then she raised the tire iron up high over her head.

"Waaaiitt! *Nooo!*"

Andrea brought it down *hard* on Mark's right kneecap, instantly busting it. He screamed so high-pitched that it was a wonder that the windows of the cars that were inside didn't shatter. Andrea busted his other kneecap then she dropped the tire iron.

"Okay, Mark. All is forgiven," Andrea said, taking steps back away from him.

Mark was crying his eyes out. Being tied up prevented him from even grabbing and cradling his busted knees.

Andrea looked at Tim, who stood by quietly, waiting for her word.

"What the fuck Andrea?" Mark cried, in so much pain that he wished for death.

"Does that hurt, Mark?" she asked him.

Mark opened his eyes. "Yes, it fucking hurts you bitch!"

"Oh. Okay. Now I'm a fucking bitch again?"

"No, no, no! Wait! I didn't mean that! I swear!" Mark capped.

"Too late, stupid ass." Andrea looked at Tim again. "Crush his bitch ass, babe."

"Andrea *nooo!*"

Tim hit the lever and made the heavy engine drop. It landed on Mark's upper half, instantly smashing him under it. His screaming and crying stopped right away. His legs and feet spasmed, kicking and trembling from the nerves inside of them still going haywire. Seconds later, they both went limp.

Cassie's sobbing brought their attention from the dead woman beater to her. Andrea walked over to her. She tried to scoot away from Andrea, but her efforts were pointless. Andrea grabbed her by her hair and dragged her over to where a hydraulic car lift was that had a big body Audi A8 up on it.

"Why?! I don't even know you," Cassie cried as she was tossed under the car.

"And I'm gonna keep it like that, whore," Andrea said, as Tim went to where the lever that raised and lowered the lift was. "Nothing personal, though; I was taught to never leave witnesses, so, buh-bye, biiatch!"

Tim hit the lever and made the lift drop down and crush Cassie, silencing her forever as Mark had been silenced.

Tim looked at Andrea, checking to see if she was okay. "Bae? You good?"

She was now looking back at Mark's legs and feet again. For so long, she had waited for the day she got her revenge. It felt so good that tears filled her eyes.

Tim walked over to her and put his arms around her. "You're good, baby. He's gone; you handled yo' business, and now, we can move past this, right?"

Andrea took a deep breath and exhaled. She nodded her head then, ready to bury the horrible memories of being a victim, and finish being trained to be a boss.

"I'm good," she then said, clearing her throat to keep her voice from breaking. "Let's get out of here."

"You go to the whip; I'll clean up, okay? Tim said.

Andrea shook her head. "We came here together; we leave out together. I am with you, Tim."

He smiled warmly at her, falling for the beautiful innocent ride or die chick even harder. He wished so badly he had found her sooner, but better late, than never.

"Okay, gorgeous. Find anything flammable and let's burn this bitch to the ground," he told her.

They grabbed cans of gas, motor oil, and other flammable liquids. They doused everything they could, then Tim rigged an old metal control panel with frayed wiring inside to start sparking. He lit up some old newspapers then hurried with Andrea towards the door. He tossed the burning paper to where a puddle of gas was, and it instantly ignited a massive fire that moved like it had a mind of its own.

They ran and jumped back into Andrea's Range Rover. Andrea slammed it into drive and mashed the gas, peeling off right as the cars inside began exploding, one by one, turning the garage into one big ball of fire.

Chapter 18

The following day, Bunz sat on her bed watching WGN news replay the reports of the brutal murders on Lennox. A young beautiful African American female wearing a bullet-proof vest that said '*Illinois State Police*' on it stood on the scene with the reporter and spoke on what was known so far. Next to the young chick was an Asian woman that wore the same Illinois State Police gear.

"This has cartel written all over it. The use of the weaponry, the brazenness, and the ruthlessness of it all is only seen by drug cartels, and for the last few years, as more immigrants have entered the United States, more criminals have come along as well, which includes gangbangers from other countries, and of course, cartels and other dangerous organizations. The mannerisms used in murdering these young men is the work of those who had perfected killing, and have no regards for human life, whatsoever. I will keep you updated as the investigation continues."

Bunz smirked to herself. She reached her iPhone up and made a call that was answered in three rings.

"Jones speaking," answered a woman.

"The camera *loves* you, girl," Bunz said, speaking to the state trooper that she had paid *very* handsomely to spin the report to ensure that no investigations ever came her or any of her people's way.

Yvette laughed, "I sure hope so. You all okay?"

"Yep. Had a little chat about *hood etiquette* with the guy. I'm sure there will *never* be another issue with him again," Bunz told Yvette, as the news channel went on to do a segment for a different report about a '*dismembered body found at Belvidere Park*', something that Bunz made sure she tuned in on to see the identity of who was '*found*'.

The female trooper that had been on the TV was a dear friend of Eric's, along with her Vietnamese partner. They handled things for him when he needed a little more muscle, and in return, he handled things for them when they needed work done off the books.

"I'm sure of that, too, girl. Gimme a holla when you need us, fam," Yvette said.

"Yep! Deuces, shortie!" Bunz replied, then ended the call.

She got up and went to shower so she could get ready for her day. She had an important meeting to get to, and deep inside, she dreaded it. It was a meeting that was likely going to make tempers flare, and maybe even cause a big explosion, but it was a necessary one.

After she showered, Bunz got dressed to look as professional as possible, but still sexy and classy at the same time. She donned a deep green Dolce & Gabbana skirt suit, with a white blouse, coffee-brown pantyhose and gold pumps on her feet. She broke out a pair of gold Cartier frames that matched her gold Cartier jewelry. She put her golden dreads up into a wrapped bun on the top of her head, applied a little makeup, then she spritzed on some perfume.

She checked herself in the full-body mirror. At first, she smiled at herself, loving how good she looked but then her mind went to Eric. He absolutely loved when she dressed like a professional boss-type chick. He loved a ghetto girl, but to him, there was nothing sexier than a hood chick in a skirt suit that loved shooting guns and fighting. Whenever Bunz got her office-girl look on, Eric ravished her until they both ran out of orgasms.

As she looked at her reflection, the memories of the love they had made her start smiling again. She did her best to remember only the good times, while the bad times of her own past fueled her to give her babies the best life she could.

Turning, she looked back at the bed. Her little boy and her little girl were both laying on their backs, side by side, looking at each other, giggling and smiling. Her eyes filled with tears, despite the smile remaining on her face. She so badly wished that her babies could have met their father. It hurt Bunz to the core that he had been taken away from them before they drew their first breaths, taken away from her, before they could become husband and wife.

Bunz made her way over to the bed and leaned down by them. She kissed them both on their foreheads and they looked up at her and started smiling and hollering their little baby yells at her, recognizing their mother happily.

"I love you, Eric Jr., and I love you, too, Mo-Mo," Bunz told them both, wiping away the tears that had just rolled down her face. "I love you both so much, and even thought daddy isn't here, he loves you from up in heaven, too."

Bunz went and grabbed her phone and made a call to Andrea to make sure that she was ready to go. They had a full day ahead of them and could not afford to be late.

***

Andrea buried her face in the pillow, screaming his name as she felt Tim's dick going in and out of her asshole, slow-stroking her backdoor like an experienced porn star that was in love with his on-camera partner. The pink pleated skirt to her new Valentino suit was up, and her off-white pantyhose were down, thong to the side. Nine inches of throbbingly hard dick up were inside of her, filling her with bliss.

She climaxed all over his thighs minutes later. Tim continued pumping in and out of her, getting closer to busting his own nut. He grunted, cursing up a storm as his nut started rising to the tip. His balls tingled and his muscles got tight. Andrea felt his cock pulsating inside of her and reaching back, she pulled him out of her ass, tooted it up higher for him, and let Tim skeet his load all inside of her ass crack, coating her booty hole with globs of hot cum.

"Fuck!" Tim cursed, smacking her ass cheek as he finished. "Fuck! This fat juicy muthafucka is *so* muthafuckin' good! *Maaan*, I can't believe it!"

Andrea laughed at him. She turned around and looked back at him, while he still was behind her. His sweaty muscular upper half had her ready to lick him up. His muscles bulged, as if he had just been working out, lifting heavy weights. His tattoos made him look like a straight thug. He was breathing hard and fast, trying to refill his lungs with air.

They both got off the bed seconds later, after a heated moment filled with sexual desire passed. They fixed each other's clothes and found themselves unable to break apart. Andrea's feelings for him were so deep. She could not for the life of her understand how they had gotten so strong so fast. The sex they had was bomb as hell, powerful even, yet their conversation was even hotter. They were friends with a lot in common. Neither of them liked being away from the other for too long, and the times that they weren't together, they stayed on each other's minds.

"Tim?" she said, looking up into his eyes.

"Talk to me, gorgeous." He wrapped his arms around her waist and pulled her to him. "What's on yo' mind?"

"Love," Andrea told him, keeping it straight up one hundred with him.

"Love, huh? What about love?"

She sighed. "How do *you* know when it's real?" she wanted to know.

"Hmmm," Tim paused and really gave her question some deep thought. After almost a minute of silence, it came to him. "Love to *me*, is when she's not only my best friend but when I can't even have good day without either seein' her or hearin' her voice."

Andrea gasped at his words. "Aww! Then... um... Tim... I think... I think I'm in love with you. Because," She paused then. Her eyes started welling up with tears as her emotions started getting the best of her.

Tim released her and cupped her face with his hands. "Take your time."

Andrea nodded her head. She took a deep breath then continued.

"I see you as my best friend and for a minute, I didn't know what that was, because until you and Bunz came into my life... I'd never had one, let alone two. The few times in between that we haven't been next to each other, I swear I was bothered by it the entire day. You are literally always on my mind, and I know it's not because I'm sprung or anything."

Tim chuckled at her.

"It's like... I can really see the greatest future with you in it, Tim," Andrea concluded.

"I can see a future with us together, too, 'Drea. One where we both are getting' money, with our people and, in the process, we put our middle fingers up to every bitch and every hatin'-ass, broke-ass nigga out there that has somethin' stupid to say about *us*."

That made Andrea laugh. "Yup. I am *definitely* in love, baby."

Right as they leaned in to kiss, Andrea's iPhone started ringing on the nightstand. She told Tim to hold that thought and ran to get it.

She saw it was Bunz calling, then saw what time it was. She answered it right away.

"Don't kill me; I'm on the way down right now."

"Well hurry up, you little snow bunny. We have a schedule to keep.

"Okay. Where are we going that's so important?" Andrea asked, making her way over to get her hand tote bag.

"You'll see," Bunz told her. "Just... when we get there, I can only ask that you keep your mind open, and don't be so quick to flip, okay?"

Her eyebrows furrowed up from the way Bunz sounded. "Uh... sure? Is everything okay?" Andrea asked.

Bunz sighed. "At some point, I hope. See you in a minute."

The call ended. Tim came up next to her and took her hand into his, seeing the look on her face.

"You okay, baby?" he asked her.

"Yeah... Bunz sounded a little off, though."

Tim nodded his head. He knew the extent of the meeting that Bunz was taking Andrea and Sonia to. It was why he did not want to be present. Though Andrea was his woman, he felt it be better if she was with the two women that had somewhat become like sisters to her. A good man was always good for a woman to have around when shit got rough, but sometimes, ladies needed each other more.

"She might just be a little tired," Tim capped. "Better hop to it, though, or Momma Bunz gon' come knockin' down elevator doors 'n shit."

Andrea managed a smile. Tim leaned down and planted a soft kiss on her lips, then he squeezed on her ass.

"Booty freak," she called him, before turning to lead him out.

"'Drea?"

She turned when he called her name. Tim walked up to her and took her hands into his. He looked down into her eyes.

"There's something I need to tell you before you go."

"Okay? What is it?"

Tim took a very deep breath, then he went for it. "I love you, too, baby. A lot."

Andrea's heart instantly started swelling in her chest. She wanted to cry tears of joy. She grabbed him and kissed him again, like she was never going to be able to kiss him again.

"When we get done for the day, Tim, you and I are locking ourselves away from the world and we are going to see who loves each other more," she told him, issuing a challenge with a mischievous smile on her face, along with hot passionate love in her mind.

"Bet," he told her, but then to himself, he thought... *as long as you actually come back to me and don't go apeshit on everybody...*

Andrea walked out in front of him, switching her ass hard, knowing he was booty-watching. She felt so dirty and sexy at the same time, aroused by the feeling of his cum between her ass cheeks. She couldn't wait to get done with whatever Bunz had planned for the day, so she could get back to Tim, and get it in again, and again, and again.

***

Outside, Sonia stood in front of her Overfinch edition Range Rover Supercharged. She was rocking a stylish Balmain dress that was black suede on the right half, while the left half was purple leather. On her feet she wore turquoise stiletto pumps and she was draped in white-gold and diamond jewelry. Her hair was flat-ironed bone straight and left to hang down her shoulders.

Bunz hugged Tracy, kissed her babies and the dogs' noses, then met Andrea and Tim as they came out of the garage, with smiling faces. Tim hugged Bunz good-bye for now then hopped into his silver Mercedes-Benz SLR McLaren. The monstrous V8 under the hood of his car roar to life out of the pipes that jutted out from under the front wheel wells, and he pulled off, blowing his chick a kiss before he headed down the driveway.

"Looks to me like you and Timmy, Tim, Tim are getting really close," Bunz said as they all hopped into Sonia's Range Rover, after peeping the stary-eyed look in Andrea's eyes as she watched the Benz bend the corner and disappear.

"Close enough that not even a Trojan could separate them," Sonia joked as she put it into drive and pulled off.

She and Bunz started laughing their asses off as Andrea sat in the back, blushing so hard that she turned completely pink.

Chapter 19

Out in Waukegan's Lake Hurst shopping section, Sonia arrived at the tall hotel that was across from an old popular cosmic bowling alley/arcade. She went and parked in the rear where most of the staff vehicles were. The three ladies all donned big, oversized shades then they all got out with their designer hand bags, strutting hard like they just knew they were the shit and fuck everyone else.

Bunz led the way to the side entrance of the hotel. Before they even got there, the door opened. A young Asian woman held the door open for them to enter unseen. Bunz handed the chick two new hundred-dollar bills, then continue to lead the other two ladies to the left, where a flight of stairs would take them to the second floor.

Coming to the first room in the long hallway on the left, Bunz tapped twice on the door. There was complete silence for just over five seconds, then the sounds of the locks being undone came. The door opened a second after and a wide muscular Black man in a black suit with gold-framed Ray Bans stood there.

He nodded his head at Bunz then stepped back, giving her and the two behind her permission to enter. Thanking him with a smile, Bunz stepped inside. Andrea and Sonia entered behind her. The man closed the door and locked it behind them. He stood at the door, with his back to it.

Inside the hotel room, the smell of cigar smoke wafted in the air. Jazz music played from the old school radio that sat on one of the long wooden dressers. Two other large men in suits wearing glasses were inside, standing by the window. Sitting in a chair, wearing a burgundy Gucci suit, with mocha-colored Gucci loafers on his feet, and a leg overlapping the other, Bunz saw the Malcolm X-look-a-like that she had been in touch with for the last few weeks awaiting her.

He smiled when he saw her. Like a gentleman with manners, he stood and greeted her with a hug, and a kiss on the cheek. Andrea saw the exchange and wondered who the man was to Bunz.

The old man smiled when he saw Sonia as well. She went and received a warm hug and a kiss on her cheek also.

"Nice to see you again, Mr. Cees," Sonia said when he released her from his long arms.

"Likewise, young lady," he replied, with a voice that sounded like a saxophone players. "It's been quite a while. Hear you have been busy," he said to her, then he glanced at all three of them. "Heard you *all* have been busy," Mr. Cees then added.

"A little," Sonia replied, turning to look at Andrea. "This is Andrea; she has quickly become like a little sister to us."

"Oh…" Mr. Cees looked at Bunz with a peculiar expression etched into his face.

Bunz remained how she was, giving no indication of what was going on in her head, though she was getting sick to her stomach at what she thought was going to be the result of Andrea's reaction to what she was about to learn.

"Andrea. This is Mr. Alvin, but everyone calls him Mr. Cees; he was like an uncle to my big bro Eric, he's like an uncle to me as well and to Bunz for that matter," said Sonia.

Andrea nodded her head. "Nice to meet you, sir. I'm sorry about Eric. I really wish I could have met him. He sounds like he was a great man."

The O.G. nodded his head. "He was, Andrea. Eric was a real man, a true hustler, and treated his woman like a woman should be treated, like his queen. I know his children would have loved him *dearly* if he was still here to help raise them."

Bunz willed her eyes not to well up with tears. Any time she heard his name being spoken in an honorable way; it made her heart hurt that he was not there.

Mr. Cees looked back at Bunz. He stepped back in front of her and hugged her again. He could tell she was going to break down.

"I'm so sorry, Monique. I plead to extend my condolences once more. The funeral was beautiful."

She nodded her head. A few tears rolled down her face, but she managed to keep her emotions in check.

"Thank you, Mr. Cees. I really appreciate you for attending the funeral. I know how much he loved you, sir," she said to him.

He released her and nodded his head. He looked back at Andrea then.

"So, this is the young lady that I was tasked to see about, eh?" he asked Bunz.

Andrea's eyebrows furrowed up as Bunz nodded her head. Sonia saw the look on Andrea's face and felt her stomach begin to churn.

"Yes. This is her," Bunz told him.

"I can see the resemblance. This is one hell of a small world," Mr. Cees then said, still looking at Andrea, studying her face as if trying to compare her to something...or someone else.

Andrea's eyebrows furrowed even more. She was beyond confused now.

Bunz took a deep breath. "Andrea," she called to her, walking to her and touching her shoulder with one hand. Andrea looked at her, dying to know what the hell was going on. "There's something that you really need to know about yourself; something that I really want to tell you, and I hope and pray that you can hear this and listen with an open mind."

"Um... okay?"

Bunz encouraged her to take a seat on the bed's edge. Mr. Cees went to where he had a briefcase sitting by the chair, he had been sitting in. He grabbed it and opened it up. He took a manila file folder out and gave it to Bunz, then Bunz gave it to Andrea.

Everyone was quiet. They watched as Andrea read through the papers. Bunz and Sonia could see the facial expressions changing rapidly. They went from confused, to shocked, to angry, as she flipped through each page. The final expression Andrea had, radiated hurt and pain. Her jaw dropped as it all set in. Bunz took a deep breath. She could feel her heart pounding in her chest. She felt trepidation as a few tears ran down Andrea's face.

Sonia felt her own eyes welling with tears. She knew what was on the papers, and she knew that for Andrea to learn what she was, all at once, she knew it had to be hurting her to the core.

"No way... this... this can't be true," Andrea said, voice breaking up as her emotions began to get loose from her.

Bunz and Sonia glanced at Mr. Cees. They saw the look in his eyes. He felt bad as well, but he had done his job. He was used to such devastation when such huge revelations were revealed to lost souls.

"Andrea. Baby girl," Bunz went and sat next to her. She put an arm around her and held her, "I'm sorry you had to find out like this. It most definitely is a lot to take in all at once, but I promise you, I am here for you."

"Me, too," said Sonia, taking a seat on the other side of Andrea.

Andrea shook her head. "You knew. This whole time, you knew that... you knew that that fucking bitch... is my *sister!*" She turned her head and looked at Bunz. "You fucking *used* me!"

Bunz opened her mouth to speak, but she just couldn't find the words. She did know that Andrea was born a

Paulmatti. That she was the illegitimate daughter of Barry the Diamond Man, and Paula Paulmatti's sister. Barry Paulmatti was a *rolling* stone that did not like to use condoms.

For the remainder of her pregnancy, Bunz had started researching everything available on the internet about the famous diamond-dealing mobster. Slowly, but surely, she found blogs, social media sites, hater sites, and business journals pop up as she dug as far as she could. Bunz saw nothing but all sorts of things about him, his worth, and his past dealings with other diamond connoisseurs. She was about to give up and tap one of her connects to find a link to get her close to Paula, when she began finding old photos or some seriously outdated sites pertaining to the big Italian mob-affiliated family.

She saw Barry's daughter and his ditzy wife in his main photos, somewhat looking like he was the president of the country. She saw Paula as a child, and wished she could blow the internet up. Just as she was about to wrap up, Bunz stumbled upon an article about a lawsuit that had been filed on Barry, by a woman claiming that he was the biological father of her daughter, and she was demanding him to pay child support.

Soon after the lawsuit was filed the woman disappeared and was never found.

A photo of Andrea was provided. Bunz used her connections then to find out where Andrea had gone once her mother vanished. She literally traced Andrea's life from when she was three years old, up to the current day. She had been able to find out that Andrea had been in an abusive relationship with a man in a well-known gang and ended up being hospitalized when he nearly beat her to death.

As the months went by, Bunz had located where Andrea was living and started doing recon on her. She followed her, every day, every night. She saw where the girl worked, and one day, when she saw the restaurant needed help, she tapped into another connection to help her bypass the application process and get her right in the door, as a Japanese woman that had ties to the Yakuza. Her background was what helped her get into the door to work for Anthony DeNucci at Sapore d'Italia, but it was her connect vouching for her that ultimately got her in so that she could get close to Andrea.

It was tremendously difficult for Bunz to break the ice with Andrea at first. The girl was so broken and hurt from such a bad and painful past that she barely spoke. Only after Bunz managed a little conversation every so often and made meals for them on down time, did Andrea start opening to her. Soon, they had become friends, and Bunz felt like a piece of shit for befriending the young girl on such false pretenses. But Bunz had a mission to accomplish, and she refused to let Eric's death be let go without retribution. Andrea was the only person she saw that might be able to get close to Paula, but since bringing her to live, the plans had changed, and Bunz grew a heart that refused to allow her to put the girl in the lion's den.

"Drea, please, try to understand," said Sonia, rubbing the small of Andrea's back. "Bunz was just-"

"NO!" Andrea suddenly shot up from her seat, furiously, crying her eyes out now, standing right in front of Bunz. "You fucking used me, Bunz! I have been getting used my whole fucking life and you did it *again*!"

Bunz went to speak. "Andrea, I-"

CRACK!

Bunz head snapped to the right hard when Andrea's fist rocked her jaw.

"Hey, Andrea!" Sonia shouted, hopping up then.

CRACK! CRACK! BINK!

Sonia hit the floor after a hot 'n spicy three-piece combo thrown by Andrea's skilled hands came flying at her. Mr. Cees held up a hand to halt his guards who were ready to step in and restrain the girl. He knew that the physical part was coming. Andrea had been used. She was angry and was letting it out.

Andrea looked at Bunz rubbing her jaw, then at Sonia, on the floor on her ass, trying to regain her single vision back. She went and grabbed her hang bag and marched towards the door.

"Andrea! Wait!" Bunz called out pleadingly.

Sandrea ignored her and demanded the big man at the door move. He looked at Mr. Cees and got a head nod for permission to let the girl out. The guy moved to the side and let Andrea unlock the door. She flung the door open and stormed out without another word.

Bunz sighed. "Well… that went exactly how I *hoped* that it wouldn't. I feel like the biggest piece of shit."

"Don't." Sonia got helped up from the floor by one of Mr. Cees' men. "In this life, we do what we *have* to do. Whenever the girl calms her ass down, hopefully we will be able to explain that to her."

Bunz looked at Mr. Cees. "Thank you for your help. I do really appreciate everything you did and I hope that if I need you in the future, you will be there."

He nodded his head. "I will. I'm sorry again about this, Monique, but you were just trying to avenge the man you loved. In-sha-Allah, Andrea will be grown and mature enough to hear you out. Anger like that never ends well if one does not control themselves."

Bunz nodded. "I agree," she told him. "As far as the other business, Mr. Cees, I've got fifty kilos of that Grade A white girl, fresh in and ready for you, and I've still got that Afghani dog food."

The old school nodded his head with a smile. "Sounds *very* good to me. The money is available upon delivery as usual. The last shipment of coke sold so fast that it was like I hadn't even received it."

"Well, my big bro has the best to enter the country." Bunz stood up and prepared t go try to find Andrea. "See you again, Mr. Cees, and thank you again."

He nodded, standing up and hugging her. He hugged Sonia next, then grabbing their bags, the ladies left out of the hotel room and made their way back outside, hoping that maybe Andrea would be standing by the door, or by Sonia's SUV.

As Bunz and Sonia stepped out into the sweltering heat, the sound of an alarm going off got their attention. Sonia could see from where they stood that it was her Range Rover.

"What the fuck?!" Sonia shouted, when she saw that her whole windshield was smashed out. "That fucking little bitch!"

Immediately, she assumed that it had to have been Andrea that damaged her ridiculously expensive SUV. Bunz gasped, a hand clamping over her mouth as she stood shocked at what she figured Andrea did.

They both rushed over to the Range Rover, slowing down when they got close. Sonia pulled out her Sig Sauer P226 XFive and cocked it, planning to pop Andrea dead in her face when she saw her.

Bunz pulled her FN America out of her handbag, following Sonia's lead. An angry woman that felt betrayed once again by someone was likely capable of anything. Bunz wasn't taking any chances. Sonia crept closer to her SUV. She peered inside and could see a brick sitting on the driver's seat along with shattered glass. Also on the seat was a little black pay-as-you-go phone.

Bunz walked up next to her and saw it. They glanced at each other, then it started ringing. Sonia took her keys out of her bag and hit the button to disarm the alarm. She unlocked the driver's door then opened it, grabbing the phone. She looked at the screen and saw unknown number on the display. She answered it and put it onto speaker mode so Bunz could hear the call.

"Who is this?" Sonia asked, looking at Bunz, who was looking at her.

Bunz had the sickest feeling in the pit of her stomach. She was so close to puking that she could taste what she ate for breakfast.

"You know who this is, you dumb-ass bitch," they both heard Paula Paulmatti say. "You two hoes thought you could beat *me*? HA! This is what it is, stupid asses; the little bitch you tried to use to get at me, I am going to torture the *fuck* out of her, then I am going to kill this dumb bitch. There is nothing that you can do. When I am done with her, I will be coming for you, *Honey Bunz*, and this time, nobody is gonna let you bite their cock off so you can get away. Buh-bye, now, *bitches*!"

The call ended then, leaving both Bunz and Sonia with their jaws nearly on the ground. They both felt faint. Time seemed to have stopped. Their hearts started hurting in their chests. The anguish they felt for what Andrea was going to suffer through brought tears to their eyes.

As they started wallowing in fear for Andrea's life, they heard a crotch-rocket engine. They turned their heads to the left and saw the same blacked-out motorcycle that had the unknown rider that had sliced Rubio's head off coming towards them.

Bunz and Sonia immediately raised their guns and pointed at the rider. They wrapped their fingers around the triggers, ready to fire on him. But he kept coming, not even seeming to be worried about having two guns aimed at him. Bunz's hand started shaking as she itched to pop him. Sonia gritted her teeth, second away from opening fire on him.

The rider skidded to a stop a few feet away from where they were seconds later. Bunz and Sonia stood poised, still with their guns pointed at him. He killed the engine, kicked out the bike's kick stand and leaned the bike on it.

The ladies stared, wishing they could see who he was. His helmet prevented his identity from being revealed. The visor was dark, too dark to see his face.

He got off the bike and stood next to it, facing them. He didn't move then.

"You have three seconds to tell us who the fuck are you, dude, or we *will* pop yo' ass!" Bunz declared, though deep inside, she discovered that for some reason, she felt no fear of the stranger.

Sonia felt no fear either. There was something very familiar about the rider. Like she knew him or something. Her heart started racing again in her chest like she had been injected with adrenaline.

The man then reached to remove his helmet. Seconds later, he had wiggled it off and his identity was revealed. Bunz and Sonia both gasped then shrieked loudly, eyes bugging wide as dinner plates when they saw his face.

Bunz stared at the man, stuck with utter disbelief, swearing up and down that her mind was playing tricks on her. There was now fucking was that she was looking at her dead fiancé…

To Be Continued…

Lock Down Publications and Ca$h Presents Assisted Publishing Packages

Due to an increase in the price of services we have increased our prices. The prices below reflect the price increase as of 11/1/24.

BASIC PACKAGE	UPGRADED PACKAGE
$699	**$1000**
Editing	Typing
Cover Design	Editing
Formatting	Cover Design
	Formatting
	Upload eBooks to Amazon
	Upload Paperback to Amazon
ADVANCE PACKAGE	**LDP SUPREME PACKAGE**
$1,400	**$1,700**
Typing	Typing
Editing (line editing/content)	Editing (line editing/content)
Cover Design	Cover Design
Formatting	Formatting
Copyright Registration	Copyright Registration
Proofreading	Proofreading
Upload eBooks to Amazon	Set up Amazon Account
Upload Paperback to Amazon	Upload eBooks to Amazon
	Upload Paperback to Amazon
	Advertise on LDP's Amazon and Facebook Page

***Other services available upon request.
Additional charges may apply

Lock Down Publications
P.O. Box 944
Stockbridge, GA 30281-9998
Phone: 470 303-9761
Email: lockdownpublications@gmail.com

Submission Guideline

Submit the first three chapters of your completed manuscript to ldpsubmissions@gmail.com. In the subject line add **Your Book's Title**. The manuscript must be in a Word Doc file and sent as an attachment. Document should be in Times New Roman, double spaced, and in size 12 font. Also, provide your synopsis and full contact information. If sending multiple submissions, they must each be in a separate email.

Have a story but no way to send it electronically? You can still submit to LDP/Ca$h Presents. Send in the first three chapters, written or typed, of your completed manuscript to:

LDP: Submissions Dept
P.O. Box 944
Stockbridge, GA 30281-9998

DO NOT send original manuscript. Must be a duplicate. Provide your synopsis and a cover letter containing your full contact information.

Thanks for considering LDP and Ca$h Presents.

NEW RELEASES

BLOODLINE OF A SAVAGE 1,2&3
THESE VICIOUS STREETS 1,2&3
RELENTLESS GOON
RELENTLESS GOON 2
BY PRINCE A. TAUHID

THE BUTTERFLY MAFIA 1-3
BY FUMIYA PAYNE

A THUG'S STREET PRINCESS 1,2&3
BY MEESHA

CITY OF SMOKE 1& 2
BY MOLOTTI

STEPPERS 1,2&3
THE REAL BADDIES OF CHI-RAQ
BY KING RIO

THE LANE 1&2
BY KEN-KEN SPENCE

THUG OF SPADES 1,2&3
LOVE IN THE TRENCHES 2
CORNER BOY CHRONICLES
BY COREY ROBINSON

TIL DEATH 3
BY ARYANNA

THE BIRTH OF A GANGSTER 4
BY DELMONT PLAYER

CHRISTOPHER "DIESEL" HORNEZES

PRODUCT OF THE STREETS 1&2
BY DEMOND "MONEY" ANDERSON

NO TIME FOR ERROR
BY KEESE

MONEY HUNGRY DEMONS 1,2&3
BY TRANAY ADAMS

HUNGRY FOR MONEY 1&2
BY SLIMBOS

A THUGGISH PASSION
KILLAZ ON STANDBY 1&2
LAND OF DA HOOLIGANZ 1,2&3
FRESH OFF DA PORCH
BY IRA B.

COUNTDOWN OF A KILLA 1&2
GUNS DOWN, BOTTOMS UP 1&2
SEX, MURDA AND GOD
BY LO-LIFE

THE LEVEL UP 1&2
BY LUXURY KING

FO'EVA ROLLIN' 1&2
BY ASSA RAYMOND BAKER

HUB CITY MENACE 1&2
BY J. WHITE

KILLA CREW
DYING FOR LIKES
BY ARYANNA

PROBLEM SOLVED 2

IF YOU CROSS ME ONCE 6
ANGEL 5
By Anthony Fields

IMMA DIE BOUT MINE 5
By Aryanna

A THUGS STREET PRINCESS 3
EMBRACING THE LOVE OF A BOSS
By Meesha

PRODUCT OF THE STREETS 3
By Demond Money Anderson

STANDING ON HER BUSINESS
BY DG SANTANA

GET IT IN SLUGS 1&2
B. STALLS

CORNER BOYS 2
By Corey Robinson

THE MURDER QUEENS 6&7
By Michael Gallon

CITY OF SMOKE 3
By Molotti

CONFESSIONS OF A DOPEBOY
By Nicholas Lock

TENDER
BY KHUFU

CHRISTOPHER "DIESEL" HORNEZES

THA TAKEOVER
By Keith Chandler

BETRAYAL OF A G 2
By Ray Vinci

CRIME BOSS 4
By Playa Ray

Coming Soon from Lock Down Publications/Ca$h Presents

RAN OFF ON THE PLUG 2 by **PAPER BOI RARI**
STREET REDEMPTION by **TONY DANIELS**
SAVAGE FAMILY EMPIRE by **PRINCE TAUHID**
BAD BITCHES WIT' GUNZ by **DIESEL**
THE SINGLE LADIES by **DIESEL**
COKE BY THE TRUCKLOAD by **DIESEL**
PROBLEM SOLVED by **DIESEL**
TIPPIN' THE SCALES by **DIESEL**
OPPS CRY TOO by **SAYNOMORE**
A GANGSTA'S KARMA by **FLAME**

AVAILABLE NOW

RESTRAINING ORDER 1 & 2
By **CA$H & Coffee**

LOVE KNOWS NO BOUNDARIES 1-3
By **Coffee**

RAISED AS A GOON I, II, III & IV
BRED BY THE SLUMS I, II, III
BLAST FOR ME I & II
ROTTEN TO THE CORE I II III
A BRONX TALE I, II, III
DUFFLE BAG CARTEL I II III IV V VI
HEARTLESS GOON I II III IV V
A SAVAGE DOPEBOY I II
DRUG LORDS I II III
CUTTHROAT MAFIA I II
KING OF THE TRENCHES
By **Ghost**

LAY IT DOWN I & II
LAST OF A DYING BREED I II
BLOOD STAINS OF A SHOTTA I & II III
By **Jamaica**

LOYAL TO THE GAME I II III
LIFE OF SIN I, II III
By **TJ & Jelissa**

IF LOVING HIM IS WRONG…I & II
LOVE ME EVEN WHEN IT HURTS I II III
By **Jelissa**

PROBLEM SOLVED 2

PUSH IT TO THE LIMIT
By **Bre' Hayes**

BLOODY COMMAS I & II
SKI MASK CARTEL I, II & III
KING OF NEW YORK I II, III IV V
RISE TO POWER I II III
COKE KINGS I II III IV V
BORN HEARTLESS I II III IV
KING OF THE TRAP I II
By **T.J. Edwards**

WHEN THE STREETS CLAP BACK I & II III
THE HEART OF A SAVAGE I II III IV
MONEY MAFIA I II
LOYAL TO THE SOIL I II III
By **Jibril Williams**

A DISTINGUISHED THUG STOLE MY HEART I - III
LOVE SHOULDN'T HURT I II III IV
RENEGADE BOYS 1-4
PAID IN KARMA 1-3
SAVAGE STORMS 1-3
AN UNFORESEEN LOVE 1-3
BABY, I'M WINTERTIME COLD 1-3
A THUG'S STREET PRINCESS 1&2
By **Meesha**

CUM FOR ME 1-8
An LDP Erotica Collaboration

BLOOD OF A BOSS 1-5
SHADOWS OF THE GAME
TRAP BASTARD
By **Askari**

CHRISTOPHER "DIESEL" HORNEZES

A GANGSTER'S CODE 1-3
A GANGSTER'S SYN 1-3
THE SAVAGE LIFE 1-3
CHAINED TO THE STREETS 1-3
BLOOD ON THE MONEY 1-3
A GANGSTA'S PAIN 1-3
BEAUTIFUL LIES AND UGLY TRUTHS
CHURCH IN THESE STREETS
By **J-Blunt**

THE STREETS BLEED MURDER 1-3
THE HEART OF A GANGSTA 1-3
By **Jerry Jackson**

WHEN A GOOD GIRL GOES BAD
By **Adrienne**

THE COST OF LOYALTY 1-3
By **Kweli**

BRIDE OF A HUSTLA 1-3
THE FETTI GIRLS 1-3
CORRUPTED BY A GANGSTA 1-4
BLINDED BY HIS LOVE
THE PRICE YOU PAY FOR LOVE 1-3
DOPE GIRL MAGIC 1-3
By **Destiny Skai**

A KINGPIN'S AMBITION
A KINGPIN'S AMBITION II
I MURDER FOR THE DOUGH
By **Ambitious**

A DOPEBOY'S PRAYER
By **Eddie "Wolf" Lee**

PROBLEM SOLVED 2

TRUE SAVAGE 1-7
DOPE BOY MAGIC 1-3
MIDNIGHT CARTEL 1-3
CITY OF KINGZ 1&2
NIGHTMARE ON SILENT AVE
THE PLUG OF LIL MEXICO 1&2
CLASSIC CITY
By **Chris Green**

LOVE & CHASIN' PAPER
By **Qay Crockett**

THE KING CARTEL 1-3
By **Frank Gresham**

THESE NIGGAS AIN'T LOYAL 1-3
By **Nikki Tee**

GANGSTA SHYT 1-3
By **CATO**

THE ULTIMATE BETRAYAL
By **Phoenix**

BOSS'N UP 1-3
By **Royal Nicole**

I LOVE YOU TO DEATH
By **Destiny J**

BROOKLYN HUSTLAZ
By **Boogsy Morina**

GANGSTA CITY
By **Teddy Duke**

CHRISTOPHER "DIESEL" HORNEZES

TO DIE IN VAIN
SINS OF A HUSTLA
By **ASAD**

I RIDE FOR MY HITTA
I STILL RIDE FOR MY HITTA
By **Misty Holt**

A GANGSTER'S REVENGE 1-4
THE BOSS MAN'S DAUGHTERS 1-5
A SAVAGE LOVE 1&2
BAE BELONGS TO ME 1&2
A HUSTLER'S DECEIT 1-3
WHAT BAD BITCHES DO 1-3
SOUL OF A MONSTER 1-3
KILL ZONE
A DOPE BOY'S QUEEN 1-3
TIL DEATH 1-3
IMMA DIE BOUT MINE 1-5
By **Aryanna**

BROOKLYN ON LOCK 1 & 2
By **Sonovia**

A DRUG KING AND HIS DIAMOND 1-3
A DOPEMAN'S RICHES
HER MAN, MINE'S TOO 1&2
CASH MONEY HO'S
THE WIFEY I USED TO BE 1&2
PRETTY GIRLS DO NASTY THINGS
By **Nicole Goosby**

THE STREETS ARE CALLING
By **Duquie Wilson**

PROBLEM SOLVED 2

LIPSTICK KILLAH 1-3
CRIME OF PASSION 1-3
FRIEND OR FOE 1-3
By **Mimi**

TRAPHOUSE KING 1-3
KINGPIN KILLAZ 1-3
STREET KINGS 1&2
PAID IN BLOOD 1&2
CARTEL KILLAZ 1-3
DOPE GODS 1&2
By **Hood Rich**

STEADY MOBBN' 1-3
THE STREETS STAINED MY SOUL 1-3
By **Marcellus Allen**

WHO SHOT YA 1-3
SON OF A DOPE FIEND 1-4
HEAVEN GOT A GHETTO 1&2
SKI MASK MONEY 1&2
By **Renta**

GORILLAZ IN THE BAY 1-4
TEARS OF A GANGSTA 1/&2
3X KRAZY 1&2
STRAIGHT BEAST MODE 1&2
By **DE'KARI**

TRIGGADALE 1-3
MURDA WAS THE CASE 1-3
By **Elijah R. Freeman**

MARRIED TO A BOSS 1-3
By **Destiny Skai & Chris Green**

CHRISTOPHER "DIESEL" HORNEZES

SLAUGHTER GANG 1-3
RUTHLESS HEART 1-3
By **Willie Slaughter**

GOD BLESS THE TRAPPERS 1-3
THESE SCANDALOUS STREETS 1-3
FEAR MY GANGSTA 1-5
THESE STREETS DON'T LOVE NOBODY 1-2
BURY ME A G 1-5
A GANGSTA'S EMPIRE 1-4
THE DOPEMAN'S BODYGAURD 1&2
THE REALEST KILLAZ 1-3
THE LAST OF THE OGS 1-3
By **Tranay Adams**

KINGZ OF THE GAME 1-7
CRIME BOSS 1-4
By **Playa Ray**

FUK SHYT
By **Blakk Diamond**

DON'T F#CK WITH MY HEART 1&2
By **Linnea**

ADDICTED TO THE DRAMA 1-3
IN THE ARM OF HIS BOSS
By **Jamila**

LOYALTY AIN'T PROMISED 1&2
By **Keith Williams**

FOREVER GANGSTA 1&2
GLOCKS ON SATIN SHEETS 1&2
By **Adrian Dulan**

PROBLEM SOLVED 2

YAYO 1-4
A SHOOTER'S AMBITION 1&2
BRED IN THE GAME
By **S. Allen**

TRAP GOD 1-3
RICH $AVAGE 1-3
MONEY IN THE GRAVE 1-3
CARTEL MONEY
By **Martell Troublesome Bolden**

TOE TAGZ 1-4
LEVELS TO THIS SHYT 1&2
IT'S JUST ME AND YOU
By **Ah'Million**

KINGPIN DREAMS 1-3
RAN OFF ON DA PLUG
By **Paper Boi Rari**

THE STREETS MADE ME 1-3
By **Larry D. Wright**

CONFESSIONS OF A GANGSTA 1-4
CONFESSIONS OF A JACKBOY 1-3
CONFESSIONS OF A HITMAN
By **Nicholas Lock**

I'M NOTHING WITHOUT HIS LOVE
SINS OF A THUG
TO THE THUG I LOVED BEFORE
A GANGSTA SAVED XMAS
IN A HUSTLER I TRUST
By **Monet Dragun**

CHRISTOPHER "DIESEL" HORNEZES

QUIET MONEY 1-3
THUG LIFE 1-3
EXTENDED CLIP 1&2
A GANGSTA'S PARADISE
By **Trai'Quan**

CAUGHT UP IN THE LIFE 1-3
THE STREETS NEVER LET GO 1-3
By **Robert Baptiste**

NEW TO THE GAME 1-3
MONEY, MURDER & MEMORIES 1-3
By **Malik D. Rice**

THE LIFE OF A HOOD STAR
By **Ca$h & Rashia Wilson**

THE STREETS WILL NEVER CLOSE 1-4
By **K'ajji**

LIFE OF A SAVAGE 1-4
A GANGSTA'S QUR'AN 1-4
MURDA SEASON 1-3
GANGLAND CARTEL 1-3
CHI'RAQ GANGSTAS 1-4
KILLERS ON ELM STREET 1-3
JACK BOYZ N DA BRONX 1-3
A DOPEBOY'S DREAM 1-3
JACK BOYS VS DOPE BOYS 1-3
COKE GIRLZ
COKE BOYS
SOSA GANG 1&2
BRONX SAVAGES
BODYMORE KINGPINS
BLOOD OF A GOON
By **Romell Tukes**

PROBLEM SOLVED 2

CREAM 2-3
THE STREETS WILL TALK
By **Yolanda Moore**

CONCRETE KILLA 1-3
VICIOUS LOYALTY 1-3
By **Kingpen**

THE ULTIMATE SACRIFICE 1-6
KHADIFI
IF YOU CROSS ME ONCE 1-5
ANGEL 1-4
IN THE BLINK OF AN EYE
By **Anthony Fields**

NIGHTMARES OF A HUSTLA 1-3
BLOOD AND GAMES 1&2
By **King Dream**

HARD AND RUTHLESS 1&2
MOB TOWN 251
THE BILLIONAIRE BENTLEYS 1-3
REAL G'S MOVE IN SILENCE
By **Von Diesel**

MOB TIES 1-7
SOUL OF A HUSTLER, HEART OF A KILLER 1-3
GORILLAZ IN THE TRENCHES
By **SayNoMore**

BODYMORE MURDERLAND 1-3
THE BIRTH OF A GANGSTER 1-4
By **Delmont Player**

FOR THE LOVE OF A BOSS 1&2
By **C. D. Blue**

KILLA KOUNTY 1-5
By **Khufu**

MOBBED UP 1-4
THE BRICK MAN 1-5
THE COCAINE PRINCESS 1-10
STEPPERS 1-3
SUPER GREMLIN 1-4
By **King Rio**

MONEY GAME 1&2
By **Smoove Dolla**

A GANGSTA'S KARMA 1-4
By **FLAME**

KING OF THE TRENCHES 1-3
By **GHOST & TRANAY ADAMS**

QUEEN OF THE ZOO 1&2
By **Black Migo**

GRIMEY WAYS 1-3
BETRAYAL OF A G
By **Ray Vinci**

XMAS WITH AN ATL SHOOTER
By **Ca$h & Destiny Skai**

KING KILLA 1&2
By **Vincent "Vitto" Holloway**

BETRAYAL OF A THUG 1&2
By **Fre$h**

PROBLEM SOLVED 2

THE MURDER QUEENS 1-6
By **Michael Gallon**

FOR THE LOVE OF BLOOD 1-4
By **Jamel Mitchell**

HOOD CONSIGLIERE 1&2
NO TIME FOR ERROR
By **Keese**

PROTÉGÉ OF A LEGEND 1&2
LOVE IN THE TRENCHES 1&2
By **Corey Robinson**

THE PLUG'S RUTHLESS DAUGHTER 1&2
By **Tony Daniels**

BORN IN THE GRAVE 1-3
CRIME PAYS 1&2
By **Self Made Tay**

MOAN IN MY MOUTH
By **XTASY**

TORN BETWEEN A GANGSTER AND A
GENTLEMAN
By **J-BLUNT & Miss Kim**

HERE TODAY GONE TOMORROW 1&2
By **Fly Rock**

PILLOW PRINCESS
By **S. Hawkins**

SANCTIFIED AND HORNY
by **XTASY**

CHRISTOPHER "DIESEL" HORNEZES

WOMEN LIE MEN LIE 1-4
FIFTY SHADES OF SNOW 1-3
STACK BEFORE YOU SPLURGE
GIRLS FALL LIKE DOMINOES
NAÏVE TO THE STREETS
By **ROY MILLIGAN**

LOYALTY IS EVERYTHING 1-3
CITY OF SMOKE 1&2
By **Molotti**

THE BUTTERFLY MAFIA 1-4
SALUTE MY SAVAGERY 1&2
By **Fumiya Payne**

THE LANE 1&2
By **Ken-Ken Spence**

THE PUSSY TRAP 1-5
By **Nene Capri**

DIRTY DNA
By **Blaque**

BOOKS BY LDP'S CEO, CA$H

TRUST IN NO MAN
TRUST IN NO MAN 2
TRUST IN NO MAN 3
BONDED BY BLOOD
SHORTY GOT A THUG
THUGS CRY
THUGS CRY 2
THUGS CRY 3
TRUST NO BITCH
TRUST NO BITCH 2
TRUST NO BITCH 3
TIL MY CASKET DROPS
RESTRAINING ORDER
RESTRAINING ORDER 2
IN LOVE WITH A CONVICT
LIFE OF A HOOD STAR
XMAS WITH AN ATL SHOOTER